Something evil was
inside the mirror. . . .

Jane's heart was thudding so loudly she could hear it. She couldn't move, couldn't run away. Her feet felt as if they'd been glued to the floor.

She opened her mouth to call for help, but no sound came out.

The figure came closer, toward the surface of the mirror.

It was dressed in filmy white, and it seemed to be dancing, swaying back and forth as it moved toward her through the mist.

And then it leaned forward, beckoning to her.

Jane's blood ran cold. It was the witch.

Find out where the evil will strike next at

DOOMSDAY
MALL

Look for these books:

#1 The Dollhouse

#2 The Hunt

#3 The Beast

#5 The Vampire

#6 The Jungle

DOOMSDAY MALL

The Witch

Bebe Faas Rice

BANTAM BOOKS
NEW YORK · TORONTO · LONDON · SYDNEY · AUCKLAND

RL 4, 008-012

THE WITCH
A Bantam Book / January 1996

Produced by Daniel Weiss Associates, Inc.
33 West 17th Street
New York, NY 10011

Cover art by Jim Thiesen

ISBN: 0-553-48184-3

Published simultaneously in the United States and Canada

Bantam Books are published by Bantam Books, a division of Bantam
Doubleday Dell Publishing Group, Inc. Its trademark, consisting of the
words "Bantam Books" and the portrayal of a rooster, is Registered in the
U.S. Patent and Trademark Office and in other countries. Marca
Registrada. Bantam Books, 1540 Broadway, New York, New York 10036.

PRINTED IN THE UNITED STATES OF AMERICA

OPM   0 9 8 7 6 5 4 3 2 1

In medieval Europe, witchcraft was believed to be harmful sorcery involving evil charms and spells. Thousands of innocent people were tried and killed for this alleged crime.

Of these, forty were executed in the English colonies of North America. Damaris Pearson was not one of them. She is entirely fictional.

WELCOME TO
DOOMSDAY MALL . . .

. . . where kids love to hang out, where stores are always packed, where fun is guaranteed.

And where evil awaits.

Evil you can't see until it's too late.

Evil that lies buried with the deadly secret of Doomsday Mall.

And until the secret is revealed, the horror will never end.

You Are Here

Upper Level

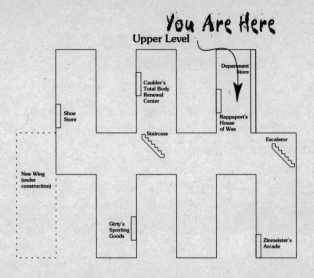

Caulder's Total Body Renewal Center

Shoe Store

Department Store

Rappaport's House of Wax

Staircase

Escalator

New Wing (under construction)

Girty's Sporting Goods

Zinmeister's Arcade

Lower Level

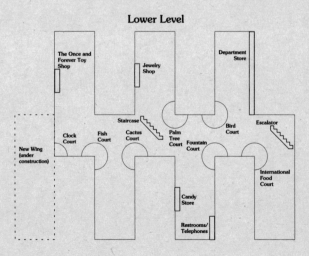

The Once and Forever Toy Shop

Jewelry Shop

Department Store

Staircase

Palm Tree Court

Bird Court

Escalator

New Wing (under construction)

Clock Court

Fish Court

Cactus Court

Fountain Court

Candy Store

Restrooms/ Telephones

International Food Court

Prologue

None of the villagers had ever seen a witch-hanging before.

The year before, two old women had been accused of witchcraft, but neither had been executed. No one could prove them guilty of evil.

It was different this time. Judge Matthews was in charge.

Judge Matthews, the sternest, most respected man in the village, was determined that this witch would not escape unpunished.

The two women who had been tried the previous year had dabbled in herbs and magical ointments, harming no one. But this witch had been accused of dark and evil deeds. Of using charms and spells and waxen dolls to lame her enemies' cattle. Of bringing sudden and mysterious illnesses upon the children of their houses.

"Give her the trial by water," the judge commanded.

"It's an ancient and sure way of testing for witchcraft."

The witch had been cross-tied, thumb to toe. Then, together with her black cat, she'd been sewn up in a sack and thrown into the pond.

"If she sinks, she's innocent," the judge told the villagers, who were eagerly watching. "But if she floats, it proves that she is indeed a witch."

The crowd edged forward, jostling one another for the best views out over the pond. There was a moment of silence, then a low murmur swept through the waiting onlookers.

The witch, in her sack, was floating. Not only floating, but bobbing like a cork across the surface of the water. If a long, sturdy rope had not been tied firmly about the sack, she might have skimmed over the pond to the opposite shore and escaped.

The rope had been the judge's idea. Judge Matthews always thought of everything.

And now the witch would hang for her crimes, here on Hangman's Hill.

No one ever came up here, except to watch a hanging. There was something . . . wrong . . . about the hill. Everyone sensed that.

The Indian tribes who had roamed this area long before the arrival of the colonists said the hill was evil. Haunted.

Maybe that was why the early settlers had built a crude gallows up here and called the place Hangman's Hill.

Now the entire village crowded around the creaking gallows to see the witch hang.

She was young and beautiful, with green eyes—the mark of a witch!—and long black hair. Her hands were bound in front of her, but even so, the villagers closest to the gallows stepped back fearfully, holding up their hands in a sign that warded off the evil eye, as the witch passed.

The crowd began to chant. "Witch! Witch! Witch!"

The black cat, who had been following his mistress closely, hissed. His eyes flashed.

The witch turned to ascend the stairs to the gallows, then raised her bound hands and pointed accusingly at the crowd.

"I curse my accusers," she said, "but especially he who brings about my death. I shall come back from the grave to destroy his children!"

The black cat died on the gallows, next to his mistress.

One

Jane Hanifin peered down the main corridor of the mall.

"I love this place," she said. "It's got everything. Shops, restaurants, and now—"

"And now it even has a wax museum," her twin brother, Jeremy, said, finishing her sentence for her, as usual. "I can't wait to see it."

"It's up ahead," Jane said, pointing. "Across from the department store. I checked the big map of the mall when we came in."

The twelve-year-old Hanifin twins looked as much alike as a boy and a girl could. They had the same straight, molasses-colored hair, streaked by the sun. The same light brown eyes. And the same long, skinny legs.

They'd always shared everything, too—toys, games, books. Even their best friend, Sam. Sam, who was also twelve, was a little shorter than the twins but squarely built, with black curly hair and dark eyes.

He hurried after Jane and Jeremy, sidestepping a young mother pushing a stroller. "I've never been in a wax museum before," he said. "But after hearing about all the ones you've visited, I sort of feel like I have."

Jane and Jeremy loved wax museums. They loved the dioramas with lifelike wax figures locked in their poses like real people caught in a game of freeze tag. Whenever the twins traveled with their parents, they always visited the local wax museum. Most large cities had one, they discovered. Such as the one in Los Angeles that showed movie stars in their most famous roles. The one in Atlanta with its *Gone With the Wind* scenes of the Civil War. And the big one in San Antonio that told the story of the battle of the Alamo.

But their all-time favorite was Madame Tussaud's, in London, England. It was the oldest and best wax museum they'd ever visited. Jeremy, who loved mystery stories and planned to be a detective someday, had been fascinated by the Chamber of Horrors and had told Sam about it many times. But the statues of famous and sinister-looking murderers had frightened Jane.

"I read in the newspaper that this wax museum has a Chamber of Horrors, too, just like in Madame Tussaud's," Sam said as they walked toward the Cactus Court. Sam read a lot of newspapers. He read a lot of everything.

5

"A Chamber of Horrors?" Jeremy echoed. "Cool!"

"Oh, no!" Jane moaned. "I don't think I want to see it."

"It's supposed to be good," Sam said. "That's where they put that local witch-hanging scene, the one Suzanne Matthews keeps talking about. She's so proud that her ancestor is in it. She says he was the judge at the witch trial."

Jane tossed back her brown hair and made a face. "That sounds like something Suzanne would be proud of—some old relative who went around *hanging* people!"

"Well, you know how stuck up Suzanne is about her family," Jeremy said. "She thinks they're better than everyone else just because they're rich."

Jane rolled her eyes. "She's such a jerk."

"The wax statue is supposed to look just like the judge," Sam added. "Suzanne says it was modeled after an old family portrait."

"I bet she's talking about that painting they've got hanging over the fireplace in their living room," Jane said. "You know, the one of the mean-looking old guy in the white wig."

Sam nodded. "Yeah, that's the one."

Jane snickered and elbowed her twin. "Do you remember when she had the whole class over for her birthday last year?"

A grin spread over Jeremy's face.

"And *somebody* tried to use the painting for the Pin the Tail on the Donkey game?"

"Suzanne was so mad at you, Jeremy, she wouldn't speak to you for days," Sam said, shaking his head.

"Yeah, too bad she got over it," Jeremy said with a sigh. "Oh, well, it was fun while it lasted."

"If that old man in the painting was the judge," Jane said, "I'm sure glad I didn't live back in those days."

Jane thought back to the picture she'd seen in Suzanne's house. The long-ago painter had managed to capture Judge Matthews's character. The cold, glaring eyes. The thin lips, pressed together in a holier-than-thou expression. The merciless set of his jaw. If he'd been *her* relative, she would have been ashamed to admit it.

They were passing the Cactus Court now. The mall had several courts, all built around different themes. This one was supposed to suggest a desert scene in the American Southwest, with dozens of cactus plants.

The three friends turned into a wide, well-lit corridor and found themselves by the main staircase.

"The museum's upstairs," Sam said. "Right up there."

The museum was large, wider than any of the surrounding stores, and was fronted in fake red brick. White wooden columns flanked each side of the entry. A beautifully lettered sign hung over the door: RAPPAPORT'S HOUSE OF WAX.

"It looks nice, doesn't it?" Jane asked. "Like a real museum."

When they pushed the door open, a little bell jangled, and a middle-aged woman with graying hair looked up from her desk. Her name tag identified her as Mrs. Hibbs.

After the three paid for their tickets, Mrs. Hibbs fumbled around on her desk and held up a map for each of them. "The museum has a number of rooms in each section. This will show you what's in each one. If you have any questions, Mr. Thatcher over there will be glad to help."

A large, heavyset man in a blue uniform was standing by a doorway marked WELCOME TO YESTERDAY. He smiled and touched a finger to the brim of his cap in a salute.

He beckoned them over. "This is the best place to start—with famous scenes from history," he told them. "Then go on to the This Is Today exhibit. It has a lot of famous people in it—movie stars and rock stars. From there you can go directly into the World of Tomorrow section. You'll like that one. It shows what life might be like a hundred years from now."

"Wait a minute—isn't there supposed to be a Chamber of Horrors in here somewhere?" Jeremy asked anxiously.

Mr. Thatcher winked. "I thought you'd never ask. It's at the far end of the museum, right after the World of Tomorrow exhibit."

Jeremy turned to Jane and Sam. "Let's go there

first," he urged. "Then we can work our way back through the other rooms."

"Okay," Sam agreed. "Sounds fine to me."

"I-I don't know," Jane stammered. "Maybe we should wait and see it last."

"So you can chicken out?" Jeremy demanded. "No way!"

"Yeah, come on, Jane," Sam said.

Jane sighed helplessly and rolled her eyes. "All right, all right, I'll go." She turned to Mr. Thatcher. "Where did you say it was?"

Mr. Thatcher pointed to the hallway at the rear of the room. "You don't have to go through the other exhibits if you don't want to. Just go down that hallway and turn right. It will lead you directly to the Chamber of Horrors." He touched his cap again. "Have fun, kids."

The hallway was long and dark.

Jane led the way. "Can't they afford lightbulbs in this place?" she grumbled.

"They've got them," Sam said, pointing up. "They're shaded. For atmosphere."

"Yessss," Jeremy said in a low, hoarse voice. "To put you in the mood." He laughed his Count Dracula laugh.

Jane suddenly remembered a spooky old movie she'd seen a few years earlier about a maniac in a wax museum. He'd murder beautiful young girls

9

and then dip them in wax and put them in the Chamber of Horrors.

So that's why Madame Tussaud's Chamber of Horrors— and now this one—made me so nervous! she thought.

Jane shuddered. The murderer in the movie had crept up on his victims in dark hallways just like this one.

Up ahead was an archway with a heavy red velvet curtain. A sign over the door said CHAMBER OF HOR-RORS—ENTER AT YOUR OWN RISK!

"Well, this is it," Jeremy said. He didn't sound quite so confident now.

"Go ahead, Jane. Open the curtain," Sam urged.

Jane reached out slowly, drew back the curtain, and stepped into the room.

Then she leapt back with a shrill scream as she came face to face with a caped man holding a dagger.

Two

Behind her, Sam and Jeremy burst into laughter.

"Relax, Jane," Jeremy managed to gasp. "It's only a wax statue." He took a closer look at it. "I think he's supposed to be Jack the Ripper. Yeah, here's the sign, see?"

Jane's heart was still thumping in triple time. "He looks so real," she said weakly.

She peered around the semidarkened room. Everything else looked real, too. The cracked, dark-stained stone walls. The torches flickering in their tall, iron holders. The wax people with their strange, staring eyes.

And in the airless gloom Jane suddenly felt the hairs on her arms rise.

Something evil, something terrible, was in the room.

And it was waiting.

It's waiting for me, she thought.

She glanced over at the surrounding tableaux. To her right, Marie Antoinette was mounting the steps of the guillotine. On her left, Julius Caesar was being assassinated. And in the corner sat Cleopatra, Queen of Egypt, about to be bitten by a snake.

The boys had edged past her into the room. She could hear them talking in low voices as they drifted from scene to scene.

Jane took a deep breath and let it out slowly.

Stop acting like a wimp, she told herself sternly. *Of course this place is spooking me. That's what a Chamber of Horrors is supposed to do, isn't it?*

"Hey, come over here, Jane," Sam called to her from across the room. "We found that witch-hanging scene!"

"This sign explains what happened," Jeremy said, leaning across the thick velvet rope for a closer look. "It even mentions Suzanne's ancestor, the judge."

Jane hurried over to them, zipping up her jacket. *Why is it so cold in here?*

Dim green lights illuminated the scene, casting eerie shadows on the wall and ceiling.

The witch was stepping toward the gallows, a black cat crouching near her feet. The judge was beside her, and the hangman stood ready, his hand on the rope.

Jane shivered and thrust her hands deep into the pockets of her jeans in an effort to warm them.

"Listen to this," Jeremy said. He cleared his throat

12

and began to read: "'In 1699, Damaris Pearson was accused of malicious witchcraft by a number of townspeople. After a brief and primitive trial, she was condemned to death by a jury of village elders, presided over by Judge Silas Matthews.'" Jeremy stopped reading. "That's Suzanne's ancestor."

"What do they mean by a *primitive* trial?" Jane asked.

"They had all kinds of dumb tests that were supposed to prove somebody was a witch," replied Sam. "Even a funny-looking birthmark or mole on your body could be used as proof."

"I can't believe something like this actually happened in our town," Jane said incredulously.

Sam did some quick arithmetic on his fingers. "That was almost three hundred years ago, Jane. People were really superstitious back then."

Jeremy bent forward again and continued to read. "'Legend tells us that Judge Matthews was a stern, unyielding man who took personal responsibility for the punishment of those whom he called "the unrighteous."'"

"He looks like he enjoyed punishing people," Jane interrupted, pointing to the figure of Judge Matthews. "Look at his face!"

Judge Matthews, in the form of a statue, looked even crueler than he did in the painting over Suzanne's fireplace.

In the scene, the judge, dressed in tight black

13

knee breeches and wearing a tall hat, was escorting Damaris to the gallows. The way his hand rested on her shoulder and the angle of her body clearly showed that he was pushing her. And roughly, too.

"Listen to what it says about the witch," Jeremy said. "'At her execution, Damaris laid a curse on her accusers, particularly Judge Matthews. She vowed she'd come back and destroy his children.'"

"Wow!" said Sam. "She didn't fool around!"

The wax figure of Damaris, her hands bound and outstretched before her, was pointing at what was probably the watching crowd.

Jane had always pictured witches as old and ugly. But the wax model was of a young and beautiful woman. She was tall and slender with long black hair.

"Wait a minute—there's more," said Jeremy, continuing to read. "'The figure of Damaris was modeled after a pen sketch recently discovered in the town archives. The model is wearing the actual clothing Damaris wore the day she was executed, also found in the archives. This includes the small ring she is wearing on her left hand.'"

Sam stared at the witch, his expression solemn. "I wonder why they kept her clothes. And the ring."

"Maybe they thought a relative would want to claim them or something," Jeremy suggested.

"And nobody ever did," Jane said softly. "I guess Damaris didn't have any friends or relatives. Only her cat."

She looked more closely at the display, particularly at the black cat pressed up against Damaris's black skirt. Black on black. Only a little white star on the cat's forehead and one white paw, like a sock, made him stand out against the background.

"What about that cat?" she asked, leaning over the velvet rope and looking down at the animal. "Was he really there at the hanging?"

"Yeah, I think so," Jeremy said, squinting at the sign. "Boy, it's dark in here. Wait a minute—there's a little note here at the end about it. It says the jury decided the cat was the witch's familiar and executed him too. By hanging. For witchcraft . . ."

His voice trailed off, and for a moment no one spoke.

"They hanged a *cat*?" Jane said, her voice quivering. "A poor harmless little cat?"

"Gross," Jeremy said. "Totally gross, and I don't even like cats."

"But they—the jury—thought the cat was Damaris's familiar," Sam explained.

"What's a familiar?" Jeremy asked.

"They were evil spirits who helped the witches with their magic charms and spells," Sam explained. "They could take the form of any kind of animal or bird, but most of the time they were cats. Black cats. Like Damaris's. Every witch had one."

"Sam, Sam, the answer man," Jeremy said. "What would we ever do without him?"

15

Jane barely heard him. The torches flickering on the surrounding walls made wavering, dancing lights in the cat's eyes.

Jane found herself staring helplessly into those eyes. They were hypnotic.

"Okay, we've done this room," Jeremy announced. "What's next?"

Sam consulted his map. "Let's see. That door over there leads to Murderers and Monsters of Story and Legend."

Jeremy peered over his shoulder at the map. "Cool! They've got Bluebeard and Count Dracula and the Thing from Another Planet."

Sam tucked his map into his shirt pocket and smiled. "Maybe we'll see Suzanne Matthews's great-grandmother as the bride of Frankenstein."

They drifted off toward the other room. At the door, Jeremy turned and called back to Jane, "Are you coming?"

"In . . . in a minute," she said.

She felt cold. So cold. Not just her hands but her whole body.

She tried to take her eyes away from the cat, reminding herself that he was made of wax. And yet he seemed to be staring at her intently, his green eyes glittering in the torchlight.

Staring, staring, as if he were trying to tell her something.

Three

Jane finally managed to wrench her gaze from the glowing eyes of the cat.

She ran her fingers nervously through her long brown hair. "Creepy," she said aloud. "This place is really creepy."

But before she turned to join the boys in the next room, she took one last look at the scene.

At poor Damaris Pearson, about to be hanged.

At Damaris's outstretched hand and the ring she'd worn the day of her execution.

How strange that she hadn't really looked at it until now.

If Jane held out her hands over the red velvet rope that separated them, she could touch Damaris. She could even touch the ring if she wanted to.

And suddenly she very much wanted to touch that ring.

She glanced over her shoulder to make sure that she was still alone in the room.

Her hand trembled as she reached out and ran her fingertip over the surface of the ring. It was thin. Narrow. Probably lightweight and inexpensive, even in Damaris's day. Jane felt an overpowering desire to hold it, to see what it looked like up close.

She tugged lightly, and the ring slipped off the wax finger into her waiting palm. It seemed to warm with sudden heat and to move—no, twitch—in her hand.

Startled, Jane pulled back her arm, nearly dropping the ring. Now it lay cool and still against her palm.

She shook her head, confused. What was happening?

Maybe the ring was warm from the lights shining on the wax finger. *Of course,* she thought. *That explains it.* And the twitch? Her fingers must have jerked or something.

She held the ring up closer to her eyes. She'd been right. It was only a cheap little thing. It wasn't even silver, much less gold.

The ring was a thin, light band of copper, darkened with age like an old penny. Its only decoration was a picture of a crescent moon surrounded by stars, drawn in enamel on its upper surface. On the inside of the ring was engraved a word—a foreign word of some sort.

Jane squinted at it in the dim light. What did it say? *Zebaalak.* Strange. But what did it mean?

She said the word aloud. "Zebaalak."

Suddenly she had the irresistible urge to try the ring on.

She glanced guiltily over her shoulder again. The room was still empty. She slipped the ring on her finger. It fit perfectly, as though it had been made just for her.

Suddenly Jane felt a rush of dizziness and the sensation of being cut off from the world. Of being surrounded by glass walls. Of being in a soundless vacuum.

Into that unnatural silence came a peculiar hissing sound, like a broken TV set, followed by static and distant muffled voices. They were angry and garbled, all mixed and running together, like the noise of a crowd. And she heard the faint yowling of a cat.

Jane opened her mouth to scream, but nothing came out.

Then, just as suddenly as they had come, the sounds died away, and the glass walls seemed to melt and dissolve around her.

It was warm in the room now. Warm with an odd, sour smell, like that of a musty closet that had just been opened.

Jane pressed her hands to her cheeks and tried to calm her breathing. She had to get out of there and find the boys. Maybe she was coming down with something.

She looked one last time at the wax figure of

19

Damaris Pearson, and a feeling of anger swept over her.

"What they did to you wasn't fair!" she whispered. She thought about what Damaris had told Judge Matthews: *I shall come back from the grave to destroy your children.*

"But you didn't, did you?" Jane told the wax figure. "Nothing bad ever happened to *him!* You're dead, but he and his family just kept getting richer and richer!"

"Hey, Jane!" called Jeremy from the doorway to the other room. "What are you doing? We thought you were coming."

Jane spun around to face him, hastily putting her hand—the one wearing the witch's ring—behind her back.

"Yeah," she said, "I'm coming."

"Well, hurry up," Jeremy said. "Sam and I are going on to the World of Tomorrow. We'll meet you there, okay?"

Jane nodded. "Okay."

Jeremy frowned. His eyes narrowed. "Are you all right, Jane? You look kind of weird."

"No, I'm—I'm fine," Jane assured him. "You go on. I'll catch up with you."

Jeremy looked at her again. "How come you're still looking at that witch-hanging thing?"

Jane forced a laugh. "I'm taking notes in case Suzanne gives us a pop quiz tomorrow on her ancestor."

20

Jeremy groaned. "She probably will, too. Okay. We'll see you in a minute."

When she was alone once more, Jane looked down at the witch's ring.

She liked the way it looked on her hand, but she knew she had to return it to the wax model's finger. She had never stolen anything in her life and she wasn't about to start now.

Taking a deep breath, Jane pulled the ring from her finger. It came off as easily as it had gone on.

But when she held the ring in the palm of her hand for a moment, it felt warm again. As if it belonged with her.

All she had to do was stretch out her arm across the velvet rope and put the ring back on the wax finger. But her arm suddenly felt so heavy. And the distance between Jane and the statue seemed to be growing.

She felt her feet step back toward the exit. She couldn't leave the ring. Jane wanted it more than she had ever wanted anything in her life.

She pushed the ring down into the deepest pocket of her jeans. Now it would be safe.

For an instant the green lights surrounding the witch-hanging scene dimmed.

And the eyes of the black cat flickered and glowed red in the darkness.

Four

When Jane got home from the wax museum, she couldn't believe what she'd done.

She'd actually stolen something! Something that was old and rare, too. Would the museum owners miss the ring right away? Would they suspect her?

"Are you okay, Jane?" Jeremy asked as they did their homework together in his room.

"Sure. Why?"

"I don't know. You've just been acting kind of weird today."

Jeremy and Jane could always read each other's moods. Their mother told them that sort of thing often happened with twins.

Jane wished it didn't. She didn't want Jeremy to suspect anything. Or to find out that she was a thief.

He would never forgive her for something like that. And besides, he'd make her take the ring back.

And he'd be right, she thought guiltily.

She put her hand into the pocket of her jeans and touched the ring. Immediately her feelings of guilt passed and were replaced by anger.

No! She would never return the ring. Why should she? It was hers now. It belonged to her. She would keep it forever.

She felt the blood rushing to her cheeks and noticed that Jeremy was staring at her.

"You've been really quiet since we saw the witch-hanging scene," he said. "Did it scare you or something?"

"No." Jane closed her math book with a bang. "But what they did to that poor woman was wrong."

"Like Sam said, that's how they acted back in those days," Jeremy said, tilting his chair backward and balancing on its rear legs. "They thought she was a witch, so they hanged her."

Jane's eyes flashed. "How could they do that? How could they have been that superstitious?"

Jeremy brought his chair forward again with a thump. "That was then, Jane, and this is now. There's nothing you can do to change what they did, so why don't you just forget about it?"

Jane got up from the bed and picked up her books. "I can't forget about it. And I can't believe you don't even care. I'm leaving. You'll just have to do your homework without my help for a change."

"And I thought *I* was the one helping *you*," Jeremy

said, raising his eyebrows in pretend surprise. "What are you getting so upset about, anyway?" he called after her as Jane stomped out of the room.

Jane slammed the door. Hard.

That night Jane dreamed she was back in the wax museum, staring at the witch-hanging tableau.

The strange feeling she'd had there came over her again. The feeling of being cut off from the rest of the world, trapped in a vacuum.

She heard the hissing sound again—the odd, electronic sound, like a broken TV set, followed by distant, muffled voices and the angry yowling of a cat.

The witch was walking slowly . . . slowly . . . up the steps to a scaffold.

Wait a minute! It wasn't the witch who was walking up those steps. It was her. Jane. She wasn't just looking at the hanging scene now. She was *in* it. Seeing it with the witch's eyes. Feeling it. Hearing the sounds.

She saw the wooden stairs beneath her feet. Felt their splintery roughness as she climbed them, one by one. Heard the excited voices of the people in the crowd, the ones who had accused her of witchcraft.

She was going to her own hanging.

The hangman was waiting for her. He swung the heavy noose before her eyes, taunting her.

She was trembling so hard she could barely walk, but she forced herself to move calmly. She hated the people down there who were jeering and pointing, calling her names. Witch. Sorceress.

But most of all she hated the man in the tall black hat who had condemned her to death. He was standing by the gallows steps, watching, a cold, satisfied smile on his thin lips. *Do not suffer a witch to live,* he had said.

And now she would die.

If only she could do something to avenge herself upon him. Something terrible to him—no, even worse. To his children!

She raised her bound hands and pointed to him.

"I shall come back from the grave to destroy your children!" she vowed.

The cat, her black cat, had followed her up the steps to the gallows. He hissed and meowed.

The hangman picked the cat up by his tail.

"Shall we hang this one before or after we do the witch?" he said with a snicker.

The cat clawed frantically at the air, howling as if he too were cursing his executioners.

Jane awoke with a start. Someone—Jeremy— was knocking on the door that connected their rooms.

The door opened, and Jeremy stuck his head in. The light from his room cast long shadows across the bed.

"Are you okay, Jane?" Jeremy asked anxiously. "You've been moaning. It sounded like you were having a nightmare."

Jane sat up and pulled the covers around her.

"I'm all right," she said, although she was still chilled and trembling. "I was having this awful dream, but it's over."

"Are you sure you're okay?" Jeremy said.

Jane nodded. "I'm sure."

Jane lay back against the pillows again. The dream had seemed so real. She took a deep breath and tried to relax.

On an impulse, she'd worn the witch's ring to bed that night. She rubbed it now. She could feel the raised crescent-moon-and-star design beneath her finger.

They'd hanged the cat. Jane shivered, remembering the way he had shrieked when the hangman lifted him up to the gallows. . . .

She imagined she could still hear his high-pitched cries.

Then she realized she wasn't imagining it. There really *was* a cat out there somewhere. He sounded angry, too. He probably belonged to one of the neighbors and had gotten himself locked out, poor thing.

Jane pulled the covers up around her ears to muffle the sounds. Finally she stopped trembling and went back to sleep.

Five

Mrs. Hanifin was standing at the stove stirring oatmeal when Jane came into the kitchen the next morning.

"Look what I just found on our back porch," Mrs. Hanifin said, pointing to the corner by the breakfast nook. "He must have spent the whole night out there, poor little thing. He looked half starved, and he was trying to get in."

In the corner, a black cat crouched over a bowl of milk, lapping hungrily yet daintily, his tail curled neatly about his feet.

"He seems like a nice cat. Very well behaved," Mrs. Hanifin said.

"So what are you going to do? He must belong to somebody," Jane asked, walking over for a closer look.

Hearing her voice, the cat raised his head, licked his lips, and looked straight at her through narrowed green eyes.

Jane had a sudden feeling of dizziness. The cat had a white star in the middle of his forehead and one white paw, just like Damaris's cat!

In fact, he looked exactly like the witch's cat.

Jane sank into one of the bentwood chairs at the breakfast table and stared at the cat as he walked over to her and sat down, the tip of his tail waving slowly back and forth. He stared up at her, unblinking, his green eyes unreadable.

Jane tried to steady her shaking hands. How weird! How incredibly weird! It was as if the statue she had seen in the museum had been modeled exactly after this cat.

Her mother placed two steaming bowls of oatmeal on the table. "I thought I'd run an ad to see if anyone's looking for him," she said. "He's so pretty. Clean and healthy-looking, too. He certainly doesn't look like a stray, but he's not wearing a collar, so . . ."

She drew a long breath and continued, "So if I can't find the owners, I'm afraid I'll have to call the animal shelter."

The cat reached out a paw—the one with the white sock—and batted Jane gently on the leg, mewing piteously. He seemed to be asking for something.

Jane bent down and stroked his warm, silken fur. He really was a beautiful cat. His resemblance to Damaris's cat was creepy, but maybe lots of black cats had markings like that.

"Mom," Jane said suddenly, "if you can't find his owners, maybe we could keep him."

Her mother looked at her, surprised. "You'd like to keep the cat?"

"You said when Sparky died that we could have another pet someday."

"But Jane," her mother said, "Sparky was a dog. And besides, Jeremy doesn't like cats."

"He just says that to sound macho, Mom," Jane argued. "He'll like Star. I know he will."

"Star?" echoed her mother. She smiled. "You mean you've named him already?"

"I guess I have," Jane said. "It just seems right for him."

Mrs. Hanifin looked up at the wall clock and sighed. "Your brother's going to be late again. And his oatmeal's getting cold."

"So can we keep the cat?" Jane persisted.

"Well . . . why not?" her mother said thoughtfully. "He seems like a nice one, and I did promise. . . . Okay, Jane. If you take care of feeding him and cleaning the litter box, I don't see any reason why we can't keep him."

She held up one hand. "But don't get your hopes up. I'm still going to run that ad. His real owners might claim him."

"They won't," Jane said. She wasn't trying to sound optimistic. Somehow she knew Star wouldn't be claimed.

*   *   *

As she climbed the stairs to her room, Jane passed Jeremy going down to breakfast. He looked half asleep, and they didn't say a word. Jane remembered how spooked she had been after her nightmare the night before. She was glad that Jeremy didn't want to talk about it. It was dumb, really, just a dream.

She heard him clomp through the foyer and into the kitchen. And then, even from up in her room, she could hear him yell, "Mom! There's a cat in here!"

She reached into her pocket and pulled out the ring. Damaris's ring.

She rubbed it between her thumb and forefinger and smiled. No matter how much Jeremy yelled and screamed, Mom would let them keep Star, Jane was sure. Star belonged there. With her.

She held the ring up to the light and looked at the strange word on its inside surface.

Zebaalak. What did that mean?

She'd worn the ring to bed the night before. But if she wore it that morning, too, Jeremy and Sam would recognize it. And maybe someone at school—someone who'd been to the museum—would also. She could carry it in her pocket, but if she did, she might lose it.

She went over to her dresser and rummaged around in her jewelry box. Her hand felt for her old silver chain. It was long and sturdy—just right for what she had in mind.

30

She opened the clasp and slid the ring onto the chain. Then she hung the chain around her neck, tucking it under her sweater, next to her body.

How strange, she thought, *the way it always feels warm when I first touch it.*

She put on her jacket and began to pick up her books. She heard Jeremy coming back upstairs, hitting every tread with a thump.

He stuck his head in her door and made a face. His upper lip had a milk mustache. "I can't believe it, Jane. A cat. Yuck! Next time, *I* get to pick the pet!"

"I heard you guys went to the wax museum yesterday," said Jane's friend Pam, slumping into her homeroom seat beside Jane as the first bell rang. "How was it?"

"It was great," Jane said.

"I mean—how was *it?*" Pam asked, nudging Jane and rolling her eyes. "You know, that witch-hanging scene Suzanne Matthews keeps talking about. She acts like she practically owns the museum. Was her ancestor really that important?"

Jane leaned forward over her books. "He was a monster!" she said heatedly. "He condemned this poor woman to death for witchcraft. Can you believe that? Everybody knows there's no such thing as a witch. I don't know why Suzanne thinks that's something to be proud of."

"She is *such* a pain," agreed Pam.

Suzanne walked into the classroom just as the final bell rang. She did that whenever she was wearing a new outfit she wanted everyone to notice.

That day it was a bright pink miniskirt, the color of bubble gum, with white tights and a fuzzy white sweater. Her long, naturally curly red hair spilled down her back in teeny-tiny ringlets.

She posed for a moment in the doorway, a hand on one hip, and tossed her head. Her ringlets danced.

"Gross! Gag me!" Pam whispered.

Jane felt a brief glow of warmth from the ring against her skin.

"I can't stand her," she whispered to Pam through clenched teeth.

All morning long, Jane couldn't keep herself from watching Suzanne. And each glance was like biting on a sore tooth. Jane could feel her anger and disgust building and building.

She hated the way Suzanne skulked around the edge of the gym during P.E. class. She hated how Suzanne pretended not to be in the dodgeball games until the very end, when she strutted around claiming to be one of the winners.

At the end of the last game, when the period was almost over, Suzanne seemed to loom up in front of her, running and waving her arms.

Pam passed her the ball, and Jane clutched it firmly in her hands.

And then something—something dark and sudden and unexplainable—happened. It was almost as if someone else had taken over Jane's body. She found herself throwing the ball, not at Suzanne's feet, but at her face. At that smug, smirking face.

Suzanne dropped to her knees, clutching her nose.

"Aaaagh! You broke it!" she shrieked.

Then she lowered her fingers and looked at them. "Blood! Blood!" Her shrill, high-pitched screams brought people running from all corners of the gym.

Ms. Milligan, the P.E. teacher, rushed over and jammed a handkerchief under Suzanne's nose.

"Let's get you to the nurse. You'll be just fine," she said.

"No, I won't!" Suzanne shouted hysterically through the handkerchief. "And it's all *her* fault!"

She pointed directly at Jane.

Six

Suzanne's nose wasn't broken. It stopped bleeding even before she reached the nurse's office.

Ms. Milligan returned immediately to the gym. She blew several short blasts on the whistle she wore around her neck and held up her hands for silence.

"It's all right," she called out. "Suzanne's fine. It was just a little bump, but the blood frightened her."

"What a wimp!" someone said. There were scattered mutterings of agreement.

"All right, all right!" Ms. Milligan said, clapping her hands. "Everyone on to your next class. Everyone, that is, but you, Jane. I want to talk to you."

She took Jane aside. "Suzanne says you threw that ball in her face deliberately. Is that true?"

Jane swallowed hard. "No, Ms. Milligan. It was an accident."

"Jane wouldn't do something like that on purpose," burst out Pam, who had followed close behind.

Ms. Milligan nodded. "Yes, that's what I thought, but I had to ask." She patted Jane's shoulder. "All right, Jane. You can go now."

When Ms. Milligan moved away, Pam put her hands on her hips, her eyes flashing. "Can you believe that? Suzanne blaming you because she stuck her big, fat head in the way of the ball."

But I did do it on purpose, Jane thought in amazement. *And then I lied to Ms. Milligan about it!*

Pam hurried out the door, late for her next class.

But Jeremy caught Jane by the wrist just as she was about to leave the gym.

"I saw what happened, Jane," he said in a low voice.

"It was an accident," she answered, looking down. Jeremy always said he could tell when she was lying by looking in her eyes.

"No, it wasn't," he said. "I was there. I saw it. That was no accident."

Jane looked around to make sure they weren't being overheard. Everyone else had gone on ahead. Her arm was shaking as she pulled it out of Jeremy's grasp.

"Fine, I admit it. It wasn't an accident," she said, her voice ragged. "I don't know why I did it. Something came over me. It was so weird. I just couldn't help it."

"Well, what you did was mean, really mean," her brother said accusingly. "Everybody knows Suzanne's

35

a pain in the neck, but she's not all *that* bad. I can't believe you did that, Jane."

Later that night Jane lay in a hot bath.

The chain, with the ring on it, was hanging from the doorknob. Was it her imagination, or did the copper of the ring look brighter, shinier? Or was it just the way the bathroom light was hitting it?

Jane ran her hand over the surface of the warm water, rippling it softly. Why had she thrown that ball in Suzanne's face? She'd never deliberately hurt anyone in her life. And the strange thing was that at the time it had seemed as if someone else was doing it, not Jane herself. As if someone else had taken over her body.

Before she'd thrown the ball, she'd felt so angry. So eager to hurt Suzanne.

She got out of the tub and began to towel herself dry.

Did I freak out or what? she asked herself.

She put on her nightgown and then carefully replaced the chain and ring around her neck. *At least it was only Suzanne,* she thought. *It's not like she didn't deserve it.*

Jane sighed as she entered her bedroom and looked over at the adjoining door to Jeremy's room. It was closed.

All their lives they'd talked for a little while each night before they went to bed. But Jeremy wasn't speaking to her that night—partly because of what she'd done that afternoon and partly because Star, the cat, had scratched him.

It wasn't Star's fault, exactly. Jeremy had been teasing him. He'd gotten down on the floor and barked like a dog, and Star hadn't liked it.

"It's all your fault we're stuck with this dumb cat, Jane," Jeremy had said pointedly as his mother daubed the scratch with antiseptic.

Well, it's a good thing he never stays angry long, Jane thought, eyeing her brother's closed door. Besides, she didn't feel much like talking that night, anyway.

Jane walked over to her nightstand and snapped on the light.

Star was curled up on her bed. The cat stirred and stretched lazily.

"How'd you get in here, Star?" Jane asked, putting the cat on the floor and pulling down the bedspread. "I thought the door was closed. I guess Mom let you in, huh?"

Star hissed and leapt back up on the bed again, his tail switching angrily back and forth.

"Okay, okay, have it your way, " Jane said as she crawled into bed and turned off the light. "You can stay up here if you don't snore or steal the covers."

The numbers on her bedside digital clock said 3:00 A.M. when Jane awoke with a start.

She'd been dreaming. A faint, faraway voice had been calling her name.

But was it really a dream? It had seemed so real.

Pale silver moonlight streamed in through her bedroom window. Jane sat up in bed and looked around. Everything looked spooky at night. She was glad she had the cat for company.

Wait a minute. Where's Star?

"Star?" she whispered, feeling around in the bed-covers. "Where'd you go?"

She couldn't see him anywhere in the room. But where could he have gone? The door was closed.

There it was—that sound again. Someone *was* calling her name. She was sure of it now.

Jane crawled out of bed and shoved her feet into her slippers.

She looked under the bed for Star, but it was too dark to see.

"Jane! Jane!" the voice called faintly. It sounded as if it were coming from down in a well.

Jane made her way toward the window. As she did she passed the full-length mirror on her wall.

Something white and ghostly was moving in its moonlit depths, rising up from a swirling mist.

"Is . . . is that me?" Jane said aloud in a low, trembling voice. She raised one arm and waved it unsteadily back and forth before her face.

There was no matching arm movement from the figure in the mirror.

Instead it drifted closer to the surface of the mirror.

Something was inside the mirror!

Jane's heart was thudding so loudly she could hear it. She couldn't move, couldn't run away. Her feet felt as if they'd been glued to the floor.

She opened her mouth to call for help, but no sound came out.

The figure came closer.

It was dressed in filmy white, and it seemed to be dancing, swaying back and forth as it moved toward her through the mist.

And then it leaned forward, beckoning to her.

Jane's blood ran cold. It was Damaris!

Jane could see her clearly now. The dead-white skin. The long black hair. And the cat at her feet. The black cat with the white star on his forehead and the one white paw.

Just like Star.

Or was it Star?

The cat trailed behind Damaris, leaning up against her and rubbing his head against her leg.

Damaris gestured again, and Jane felt herself being drawn toward the mirror.

Her feet moved reluctantly but steadily closer to the beckoning figure.

And then Damaris's hands reached out of the mirror toward her. They scrabbled around blindly, opening and closing, trying to catch hold of Jane.

39

In the mirror, Damaris's lips were moving. "Come to me! Come to me!" she called silently.

She wants to pull me into the mirror! Jane thought desperately, trying to resist. "No!" she managed to gasp, finding her voice at last. She took a deep breath and screamed, but it was only a muffled sound, no louder than a whimper.

The hands reached out farther. Their nails were long and pointed, like a bird's talons, and were painted a dark blood red.

Jane willed her legs to move, to back up, but they wouldn't respond. She tried to scream again, but only a whisper came out.

Damaris's groping hands closed on the sleeve of Jane's nightgown. Jane heard the sound of nails sliding over fabric as Damaris's fingers fastened on the soft cloth.

And then she was being drawn forward into the mist. Into the mirror.

In another moment she would be inside—and lost forever.

With a mighty effort, she threw herself backward, away from Damaris.

And then she was falling.

Jane felt the floor rush up to meet her, and everything went black.

Seven

"Get up, Jane. What are you doing on the floor?"

Jane opened her eyes.

"What's wrong with you?" Jeremy said, grabbing her shoulder and shaking it. "You were making weird noises in your sleep again."

Jane sat up groggily. "It's her!" she said, pointing to the mirror. "Damaris! She's in there!"

"*What?*" Jeremy said, turning around to see.

They looked at the mirror. Only flickering moonlight and the dark reflections of objects in Jane's room glimmered there.

"Damaris? In your mirror?" Jeremy asked incredulously, staring at her. "Jane—have you lost it? What are you talking about?"

Jane struggled to her feet. She tripped over the hem of her nightgown but righted herself.

"S-She—the w-witch—was just here," she stammered. "She tried to pull me into the mirror!"

41

"Jeez, Jane, you were only having a crazy night-mare," Jeremy told her. "And you were walking in your sleep again. You stopped doing that years ago."

"It wasn't a nightmare," she insisted. "Damaris was really there. I saw her. And Star was in the mirror with her."

"Star? The cat?"

"Yes. When I woke up, Star was gone. I didn't know how he'd gotten out of the room, because the door was shut. But he'd gone into the mirror."

Jeremy put his finger to his lips. "Shh! Keep it down, Jane, or we'll have Mom and Dad in here."

Jane leaned closer to Jeremy. "Star is Damaris's cat. Star is a witch cat!" she said in a fierce whisper.

"Jane, that witch has been dead for three hun-dred years. How could Star be her cat?"

Jeremy was speaking in low, soothing tones. Humoring her, Jane thought bitterly, because obvi-ously he thought she'd gone nuts.

"Didn't you notice that Star looks like the cat in the wax museum?" she asked sharply. "The white star in the middle of his forehead? The white paw?"

"C'mon, Jane, calm down. Most black cats have white patches on them somewhere."

"Then where *is* Star?"

Jeremy went over to Jane's nightstand and snapped on the light.

Star reared up from beneath the bedcovers, yawn-ing sleepily.

"There's your mystery cat," Jeremy said. "He's probably been there the whole time."

"But—but the witch," whispered Jane. "I didn't dream her, Jeremy. She was really there."

Jeremy took her by the hand and led her to the bed. He sat down beside her.

"Jane," he explained patiently, "there *is* no such thing as a witch. It's just superstition."

"Oh, yeah? Then what about Damaris?"

"There were lots of women like Damaris in those days. Someone accused them of witchcraft, and that was it. They didn't have a chance."

"But what if Damaris really *was* a witch?" Jane said. "What if I didn't dream all this just now?" She pressed trembling fingers to her cheeks. "It was so terrible, Jeremy. I could almost feel the . . . the *evil* . . . coming from Damaris."

"You know, Jane," Jeremy said, still in that calm, patient voice, "I'm sorry we went to that wax museum. You've been acting really weird ever since." He took a deep breath. "Remember when you were little? How you used to have nightmares and walk in your sleep?"

Jane nodded reluctantly.

"Well, I think you're starting to do it again. Think about it, Jane. A wicked witch in your mirror?"

"It does sound kind of dumb," Jane admitted. "But it seemed so real. If you could have seen it . . ."

"Yeah, well, nightmares always do seem real." Jeremy fumbled in the bedclothes and pulled Star, snarling, from his cozy nest. "I'd have nightmares, too, if I had to sleep with this mangy, flea-bitten thing," he said, making a face.

He set Star on the floor. The cat hissed and spat at him, then leapt back up on the bed.

"I'm going to bed before that vicious animal attacks me again," Jeremy said, standing up and yawning. "Will you be okay now, Jane?"

"Yeah. Thanks," Jane said with a weak grin.

Jane turned off the bedside light and sank back onto her pillow.

Yes, Jeremy was right—it had to be a dream. She shouldn't have gone into that awful Chamber of Horrors. The witch-hanging scene had upset her more than she'd realized.

Jane fell asleep at last.

And as she drifted off she heard a soft, musical voice chanting partly in English, partly in what sounded like a foreign language:

> Wicca, ecca, astaramus
> Wicca, ecca, tremilamus
> Darksome night and shining moon
> Hearken to the witches' rune
> East and south and west and north
> Here we come to call ye forth.

And then she heard laughter—faint at first, and then louder and louder.

Eight

When morning came, the events of the night seemed foggy and distant to Jane. All she remembered was that she'd had a weird nightmare. One that involved Damaris and Star. And that she'd been walking in her sleep.

She was embarrassed that Jeremy had seen her like that. He was treating her nicely. Too nicely. The way he always did when he felt she'd made a fool of herself.

And all day the rhyme from the night before kept repeating in her head like a haunting refrain: *Wicca, ecca, astaramus* . . .

She tried to forget it. To think of something else. But it came back in spite of everything she did.

It was almost as if somebody was inside her head, whispering to her softly.

In history class the teacher, Ms. Lubek, rapped on her desk for order.

"All right, class, today's the day we turn in our reports," she said. She resettled her glasses on the bridge of her nose and looked out over the room. "I know you've been working hard on them these past few weeks. And I'm sure I don't have to remind you that the grade you receive on your report will make up a large part of your final grade."

Jane could see Sam, in the first row, carefully remove his report from a large, stiff folder and set it on his desk. History was Sam's best subject. He'd probably get an A+ on his paper.

Next to him, Jeremy pulled his out of his backpack. It looked battered and rumpled around the edges, even from where Jane sat.

Jane looked down with pride at her report in its see-through plastic cover. She ought to get a good grade. She'd spent hours on it, even illustrating the first page.

Ms. Lubek came around from behind her desk and stood before the class, her arms folded on her chest. "Jane, would you please collect them?"

As Jane walked up and down the rows of seats, collecting the reports, she could hear the whispered chanting again:

Wicca, ecca, astaramus
Wicca, ecca, tremilamus
Darksome night and shining moon
Hearken to the witches' rune

46

East and south and west and north
Here we come to call ye forth.

It had a rhythm to it, like a rap song. It was almost impossible not to start moving in time with it.

Jane tried to close her mind to the annoying rhyme, but it kept going, repeating itself like a broken record.

She bit her lip in annoyance, but she could hardly feel it. Her face seemed strangely numb.

A feeling of unreality was coming over her. A feeling of being somewhere else. Her body was walking around the classroom, collecting reports, but a part of her was in the wax museum, looking at the statue of Damaris Pearson. Gazing into the witch's shining green eyes.

Ms. Lubek was at the blackboard talking, her back to the class, when Jane placed the reports on her desk.

It wasn't until she returned to her seat that the chanting voice stopped and she began to feel more like herself again.

But there was something on her desk, a folder peeking out from beneath her notebook. It was Suzanne's report.

How had it gotten there?

Ms. Lubek had left the blackboard and now was counting the reports. She looked up, frowning. "There's one missing," she announced. "Did anyone not hand in a report to Jane when she collected them?"

A buzz of conversation ran through the class as the students turned and looked at each other.

Jane knew she should bring up Suzanne's report, but the moments were passing quickly. She sat paralyzed in her chair. In a few seconds it was too late to explain.

"You all know, don't you," Ms. Lubek said sternly, "that anyone not turning in a report will automatically get a failing grade?"

She flipped through the reports again and looked up in surprise. "Suzanne, it's your paper that's missing. Where is it?"

"But I turned it in," Suzanne protested shrilly, tossing back her red curls. "Jane just collected it."

All eyes turned to Jane.

"Oh . . . ah . . . here it is," Jane stammered, feeling the blood rush to her face. She pulled the report out from under her notebook and carried it up to Ms. Lubek. "It . . . it got mixed up with some of my other stuff. I don't know how that happened, Ms. Lubek."

"Really, Jane," Ms. Lubek said. "You should be more careful."

"She did it to be mean, Ms. Lubek," Suzanne piped up. "Yesterday she tried to break my nose!" She glared at Jane.

"It was an accident," Jane said helplessly.

Ms. Lubek held up her hands. "We've wasted

48

enough time on this already. I'm sure it was an honest mistake on Jane's part, Suzanne. And there's been no harm done, has there?"

"If you say so, Ms. Lubek," Suzanne said with an injured sniff. "Besides, I'm not the kind of person who holds a grudge."

Jeremy and Sam were waiting for Jane in the hall after class.

"What is going on with you and Suzanne?" Jeremy asked.

"What happened just now with her report was an accident, if that's what you mean," Jane snapped.

"You can't fool me, Jane," Jeremy said. "I know you're up to something with her. Drop it before you get into trouble, okay?"

Sam's dark eyes were solemn. "Jeremy's right. You're freaking out about Suzanne. Jeremy and I have noticed it. Pretty soon everyone else will, too."

Jane rolled her eyes and sighed. "Thank you for your advice, guys. You're totally off base, as usual, but thanks anyway."

Sam raised his head and sniffed. "I think there's pizza for lunch today. We'd better get going before they run out."

Pizza was one of Jane's favorite lunches, but that day she really needed some time alone.

"I'll meet you there," she said, starting off in the opposite direction. "I have to check on my Book Week poster."

*   *   *

The art room was deserted. Jane paused in the doorway and looked around, smiling. She loved art and was good at it. She was sure she'd win first prize for the poster she'd made for Book Week.

Each poster was supposed to illustrate a famous children's book. Jane had chosen *Little Women*. She'd drawn the four sisters sitting around a fireplace, reading. It had been fun painting those old-fashioned dresses with their high, ruffled collars and full skirts.

The poster was propped on an easel, drying.

Suzanne's was right next to it. Jane's lip curled with disgust. Suzanne had chosen *Famous Fairy Tales*.

How babyish, Jane thought spitefully.

Suzanne had drawn a princess in a tower. The princess was leaning over the parapet, her long hair hanging down nearly to the ground. The hair was made of yellow yarn. Suzanne had even glued tiny rhinestones around the princess's head to make it look as though she was wearing a crown. It glowed in the light like the witch's coppery ring, which lay hidden on its chain under Jane's shirt.

She could hear the chanting again, and instantly she felt herself back in the wax museum, in the Chamber of Horrors, and in front of the statue of Damaris Pearson.

Suddenly Jane wasn't looking at the diorama. She was looking *out* from it.

She was in the wax figure of Damaris Pearson, looking out from those green glass eyes at people filing past.

It seemed so real. The hushed comments. The pauses as people stopped to read the sign that told the history of the witch trial and hanging.

A bell rang, long and loud, rousing her from her waking dream. The end of lunch period.

Jane shook her head and tried to collect her thoughts.

And then, to her horror, she realized she was clutching a pair of long, sharp scissors.

She was holding them in front of Suzanne's poster.

Nine

Jane gasped and quickly laid the scissors down on the worktable.

She nervously examined Suzanne's poster, but it was untouched, the poster board smooth and unmarred. Had the bell stopped her just in time?

Jane let her breath out slowly and sank down on one of the chairs at the table.

It was as if she had become another person. Or as if another person had come into her body.

The ring felt warm against her skin. Jane pulled it out on its long chain and looked at it.

She hadn't been imagining things the night before. The copper was looking much shinier now, the enamel brighter. It really was a pretty ring.

Jane rubbed the ring absentmindedly between her fingers. She had to talk to Jeremy and Sam, tell them everything. She'd never kept secrets from them before. Maybe they'd know what to do. Especially

52

Sam. He always had a solution for every problem.

She'd have to tell them about the ring, of course.

And then they'll make me take it back to the museum!

Her fingers paused in their rubbing motion. She held the ring up on its chain and looked at the word on its inner surface. *Zebaalak.* She repeated the word aloud. "Zebaalak."

It sounds like a charm. An incantation, she thought.

The ring wavered and shimmered before her eyes. She felt dizzy and confused for a moment.

And then she knew what she must do. She must keep the ring a secret. And no one must know that she hated—yes, *hated!*—Suzanne Matthews.

What Jane had done—in the gym, in history class, and now in the art room—had been right. The exact, correct, and only thing to do!

The bell for the next class rang, and Jane picked up the scissors again.

Lockers were slamming shut in the hallway, and she could hear the clamor of students hurrying to their classes. She knew she was already late.

She hesitated for a minute, then laid the scissors down on the table. She couldn't make herself destroy someone else's artwork. Even artwork in which the princess had a glued-on rhinestone crown and strings of yellow yarn for hair.

Never mind, said a little voice in her head. *You will not fail to accomplish the most important task: the ultimate act of revenge.*

53

Ten

"I don't see any advertisement for a lost cat," Mrs. Hanifin said after supper, looking up from the evening paper. "And no one has called about the one I ran, either. Isn't it odd that no one is looking for Star? He's such a beautiful cat."

"Oh, gross," Jeremy groaned. "I guess we'll be stuck with him, then."

Star, sitting at Jane's feet in the den, looked over at Jeremy, his green eyes slitted and gleaming.

"Be careful," Jane warned, half in earnest. "I think Star understands what you're saying."

"I doubt it. He's way too dumb," Jeremy said. He picked up a needlepoint pillow and threw it at the cat.

Star ducked, hissed, and ran over to the corner by the fireplace. He drew himself up in the shadows and sat quietly, glaring at Jeremy, his tail moving slowly back and forth.

Mr. Hanifin looked up from *TV Guide.* "Now,

Jeremy," he said mildly. "Don't tease the cat."

"Listen to this," Mrs. Hanifin said. The newspaper rattled in her hands as she folded back the page and creased it. "Someone's stolen something from that new wax museum."

Jane froze, keeping her eyes fixed on the book in front of her.

"Really?" Jeremy said, making a face at Star. "What did they steal?"

The cat hissed again.

Mrs. Hanifin peered at Jeremy over the top of her paper. "Didn't you tell me you saw that witch-hanging scene in the Chamber of Horrors?"

"Yeah," Jeremy said. "Why?"

"Someone has stolen a ring right off the witch's finger," said Mrs. Hanifin, shaking her head. "Imagine that! The ring is supposed to be very valuable, too. It actually belonged to the real witch—I mean, the woman they hanged for witchcraft—so it's very old."

Jane bent her head closer over her book. She was afraid they would all see the guilt in her eyes if she looked up.

"I remember that ring," Jeremy said thoughtfully. "Don't you, Jane?"

"Uh—yeah," Jane mumbled. "Sort of."

"It wasn't very fancy," Jeremy said. "I mean, it wasn't a diamond ring or anything. I wonder why anyone would want to take it."

"Some people will steal just about anything

nowadays," said his father, frowning and picking up the TV remote control. "It makes you wonder what this world is coming to."

That night Jane lay awake in bed for a long time. She was afraid to fall asleep. Afraid to fall into another terrifying nightmare.

But she could feel her eyelids growing heavier. She had to let them drop, and finally she fell into a shallow sleep.

Jane dreamed that something was on top of her, suffocating her.

She tried to catch her breath. Tried to draw in air. She was smothering!

She awoke, trembling, to find the black cat crouching on her chest, peering down into her face.

His eyes gleamed in the darkness. His breath was sour and hot.

She pushed him away and wiped her hands on the bedcovers. Star's fur felt dusty, as if he'd been rolling around outside. But he'd been there in the room with her all night. So where could the dirt have come from?

From a graveyard.

The words popped into her head from nowhere, and she quickly rejected them. She had to get a grip.

Still, Star couldn't stay on the bed if he was dirty. Jane tried to raise herself to a half-sitting position, so she could shove him off onto the floor, but she fell back on her pillow, her head spinning.

What was wrong with her? Suddenly she felt so weak. So tired.

"Get off, Star," she whispered faintly. "Go away. Leave me alone!"

The cat slowly walked the length of the bed, from the foot, where she had pushed him, to her pillow, his tail held high. He sat down, hunching over her, his eyes glowing and intense.

"What do you want?" Jane murmured. She felt as if she were sinking. The ring was warm against her skin.

A pleasant haze was beginning to envelop her, and then she heard the voice.

It was low and musical, the same voice she'd been hearing all day, chanting the rhyme.

Only now she knew whom the voice belonged to. Damaris. Had she known all along that it was Damaris?

Jane could hear the words distinctly now:

> By all the powers of land and sea
> As you have done, so must it be
> By all the might of moon and sun
> The work we do has just begun!

Jane tried to lift her eyelids, but they were heavy again. So heavy.

> What you have done these past two days
> Has shown your heeding of my ways,

Your willingness to serve—and now
You'll do the deed that seals my vow.

Soft laughter, and then Jane spiraled down, down
into darkness.

Eleven

"You look dead this morning," Jeremy said as they waited for the school bus.

Jane sighed. "That's what Mom said. It's nothing, really. I just had another nightmare."

Jeremy eyed her more closely. "You've been having a lot of them lately. Maybe you should do something about it. Drink warm milk before you go to bed or something," Jeremy said.

"Thanks," Jane answered, trying to sound grateful. "Maybe I will."

If only she could tell Jeremy more about her nightmare. About the voice chanting the rhyme. About Damaris.

But she couldn't. She couldn't get the words past her lips. She would just have to handle this on her own.

All day Jane was very, very polite to Suzanne. After school they both missed the first bus in order to stay late and put the finishing touches on their Book Week posters.

Jane turned to Suzanne, determined to be extra nice. "Gluing that yarn hair and the rhinestone crown on your princess made it really artistic-looking," she said. "It came out so cool."

"If you're trying to make up to me for the nasty things you've done lately, Jane," Suzanne said, looking hurt and putting a little quiver in her voice, "I forgive you. I'm that kind of a person, you know."

Jane bit her lip. *From now on I'll just ignore her,* she thought.

Suzanne and her little brother, Gordie, walked ahead of her to the school bus stop. The second bus would be coming along soon.

But when she saw the bus approaching, Jane found herself casually drifting over to where Suzanne and Gordie were standing.

Suzanne had one foot on the curb and one in the street and was hopping back and forth, talking to Gordie.

Again, as they'd been doing on and off all day, thoughts of Damaris crept into Jane's consciousness. She could almost hear the witch's long-ago vow to Judge Matthews: *I shall come back from the dead to destroy your children.*

The bus came closer.

Suzanne and Gordie were still teetering on the edge of the curb. They seemed to be arguing about something.

Some other kids were standing a short distance away, huddled around Kevin Driscoll, the class karate expert, who was acting out some moves from a kickboxing movie he'd just seen.

Good, said the little voice in Jane's head. *No one is looking.*

The bus was only a few yards away now. And suddenly it seemed so huge. So deadly.

She heard the high-pitched voice again.

Pretend to stagger and to fall
A tiny push will do it all
First the lass and then the lad
Will fall beneath the wheels—how sad!

The voice dissolved into soft, mocking laughter.

Jane shuddered. She was standing beside Suzanne as the bus came rolling toward them. Her shoulder was next to Suzanne's.

Pretend to stagger and to fall . . .

Jane felt lightheaded and removed, as if she were watching herself from a long way off. She could feel her foot slipping, her body turning toward Suzanne. All she had to do was reach out and grab on to her.

As the bus neared, the driver pressed on the horn and the bus blasted out its usual warning.

Jane broke out of the foggy, unreal state she'd been drifting into. *What am I doing?* she thought.

"Watch out!" she shouted, reaching out and pulling Suzanne fully onto the sidewalk. "You too, Gordie. You shouldn't be so close to the road."

Suzanne yanked her arm away from Jane. "Well, really, Jane!" she said indignantly. "You don't have to be so bossy! We weren't doing anything wrong!"

Gordie turned and stuck his tongue out at Jane as he clambered up the steps of the bus behind his sister.

The witch's ring grew warmer and warmer against Jane's skin on the bus ride home.

Jane, sitting alone in the back of the bus, yanked the ring up by its chain and let it hang outside her sweater. There. That was better. She could think more clearly now.

She had to talk to someone about the way she'd been acting lately, and about the ring. It had all started with the ring.

And about Damaris Pearson, the witch.

Yes, a witch. Jane realized that now. A witch who had used her power to do dark and evil things.

What if these weren't nightmares that she was having?

What if she was under a spell—a witch's spell?

Jeremy and Sam were playing catch on the front lawn when she got home.

"You're late," Jeremy said, reaching out and snagging Sam's famous fastball.

"You weren't there when the first bus came, so we went on without you," Sam said. "What happened?"

"It's a long story," Jane said. "Can you two come up to my room? There's something I have to tell you."

Twelve

The house was silent. Mrs. Hanifin was working at her part-time job in a small local bookstore.

Jane took the ring and chain off her neck as she climbed the stairs. If she kept it on, she was afraid she wouldn't be able to tell Jeremy and Sam everything.

She'd wanted to do this the day before, but something had kept her from it. That wasn't going to happen this time. She needed help. She couldn't wait any longer. What if the next time she heard the strange chanting, she couldn't keep herself from really hurting Suzanne?

Jane entered her room first, holding the door open for the boys. The afternoon sunlight streamed in through her windows, and little dust motes danced lazily in its slanting rays.

She hung the chain from a knob on her bureau, taking care not to touch the ring itself.

Sam and Jeremy sat down cross-legged on her bed. That was how they always sat when there was something important to discuss. From the expressions on their faces, Jane knew they sensed something serious was coming.

Jane pulled a chair over to the bed and sat down. She glanced around the room for the cat and was glad when she didn't see him. She didn't like the way he always seemed to hang around and listen to them.

"Hey!" Jeremy said, looking over at the ring. "Isn't that—?"

Jane nodded. "Yeah," she said. "That's what I've got to talk to you about."

Sam's eyes were huge and unbelieving. "Jane, are you going to tell us you *stole* that ring from the museum? Is that what this is all about?"

"No wonder you've been having all those crazy nightmares," Jeremy said, glaring at her. "I can't believe you did something that dumb. You're going to be in trouble, really big trouble, if anyone finds out about it."

Jane held up her hands. "Wait a minute. Just let me tell it from the beginning, okay?"

"This better be good," Jeremy muttered. "You've never done anything this stupid before, Jane." He shook his head.

"Give her a break, Jeremy," Sam said. "Shut up and let her talk."

Jane shot Sam a grateful look and took a deep

breath, letting it out slowly. She didn't dare look at the ring hanging from the bureau. If she did, she knew she wouldn't be able to continue.

"It all started with that trip to the wax museum," she began.

She told them about the ring, the nightmares with Damaris, the chanting that she heard in her head, and her violent anger against Suzanne.

Jeremy and Sam stared silently at her, their eyes wide.

"It's like someone else is in my body sometimes," she said. "That's how it was when I threw the ball in Suzanne's face, and when I hid her history report yesterday."

She paused, then added, "And I nearly slashed her Book Week poster with a pair of scissors yesterday, too, but I caught myself just in time."

"Jeez, Jane," Jeremy interrupted. "This is kind of heavy."

"Well, it gets heavier. Listen to this," Jane continued. "I'm beginning to think it's Damaris who's in my body, making me do terrible things. She hates Suzanne. I'm afraid she'll make me do something really bad. Something that will hurt Suzanne a lot."

Jeremy and Sam exchanged troubled looks.

"I thought you didn't believe in witchcraft, Jane," Sam said.

"I didn't. But I do now," Jane replied.

"Whoa," Jeremy said. "Damaris Pearson was probably just some poor girl who had a wart on her nose or something, and she had a black cat, so right away people thought she was a witch."

"That's another thing," Jane said. "The black cat. Star looks just like—"

"We've been over that before," Jeremy cut in. "All black cats look alike, sort of."

"None of this makes any sense," Sam said. "Why would the witch—if she really *is* a witch—wait three hundred years to come back from the dead to get revenge on the judge?"

"I don't know," Jane said impatiently. "Maybe it has something to do with the ring. It's been locked up in the archives until just recently."

"But why you?" Jeremy asked. "Why not someone else?"

"Because I stole the ring," Jane said bitterly. "I was the one who did something wrong. I opened some sort of door that let Damaris through."

She glared at the two boys. "Oh, what's the use? I thought you'd understand. That you'd try to help me."

"We are trying," Sam explained gently. "But you have to admit, what you're saying *does* sound pretty far out."

"Wait a minute! Wait a minute!" Jeremy held up his hands for silence. "We've got a real problem here, and I think I've figured out what started it and what we can do to stop it."

Jane sat up straight and narrowed her eyes at her twin. "Okay. Keep talking."

"First of all, about this witch stuff," Jeremy said. "I think that scene in the museum kind of got to you. That Chamber of Horrors was creepy, and maybe you freaked out, just like you did in Madame Tussaud's."

"I did not freak out!" Jane said indignantly.

"You've always been weird about witches anyway," Jeremy went on. "Mom won't even let us watch *The Wizard of Oz* on TV because you practically crawl under the table when the wicked witch does her thing."

"This is completely different!" Jane snapped.

"Jeremy's right," Sam said. "You have a pretty wild imagination about some things, Jane. This whole thing started when you stole the ring from the wax model of the witch. You've never stolen anything in your life. You've probably been feeling so nervous and guilty about it that you started imagining all the rest."

"Then what about the things I've been doing to Suzanne? How do you explain that?"

"That's easy," Sam said. "You never have liked Suzanne. Seeing what her ancestor did gave you an excuse to get back at her for all the rotten things she's done to you in the past."

"That's hard to believe," Jane said flatly.

"It's easier to believe than the stuff you've been saying," Jeremy told her. "I mean, get real, Jane. You expect us to believe that stealing the ring brought an evil witch back from her grave? And that the witch is trying to take over your body so she can get revenge on Suzanne Matthews?"

"It . . . it does sound pretty wild, doesn't it?" Jane said slowly. She thought for a moment. "But what about the ring and the way it makes me feel? I know I'm not imagining that."

Sam cleared his throat. "You just think it has power over you because you want to blame the ring, not yourself, for what you're doing."

"That could be. It does make sense when you think of it that way," Jane said. "I mean, I *have* been blaming the ring for everything, haven't I?"

She remembered what had nearly happened at the bus stop. *I couldn't really have tried to kill them,* she thought. *I must have imagined that part.*

"So all you have to do is return the ring," Jeremy was saying.

"What?"

"Return the ring, and you'll be okay."

It sounded so simple. Return the ring, and her life would go back to what it had been. But the idea only made her feel more tense and worried.

"What if they catch me? Or what if they guess I'm the one who brought it back? They'll want to know where I got it," she argued.

"No, they won't," Jeremy assured her. "A lot of kids have been going to the museum after school. Just wait until a big group has left and slip in after them. No one will ever know who returned the ring."

"You've got to do it, Jane," Sam urged. "It's valuable and it's stolen and they'll keep on looking for it. If they ever find out you took it, you'll be in big trouble. The police, the newspapers . . . you might even get kicked out of school."

Jane shuddered. She hadn't thought about that part of it. She'd been too involved in thoughts about Damaris and in the weird things she'd been doing to Suzanne.

She stood up and hitched up her jeans. "You're right," she said. "I'll go over there right now." She hesitated for a moment. "Can you guys come with me?"

Sam looked at his watch. "We have baseball practice and we really shouldn't miss it," he said.

Jeremy jumped to his feet. "I'm in enough trouble with the coach already. Come on, Sam." He put his hands on Jane's shoulders. "Don't worry," he said. "You'll be fine. Trust me."

"I hope so," she said.

She picked up the chain and removed the ring, glancing at it before tucking it into her back pocket. It looked so small. So harmless.

Jane was the first to leave the room. She almost tripped over the black cat, which was crouching outside the door.

He skittered away guiltily, like someone who had been caught eavesdropping.

Thirteen

Jane pedaled furiously through the neighborhood streets toward the mall. It was only a mile away. She, Jeremy, and Sam went there often on their bikes.

There's definitely something wrong with the cat, she thought.

He had run down the stairs ahead of them and slipped outside when they opened the front door. By the time they'd picked up their bikes, the cat was halfway down the block.

"Hey, look at him go," Sam had said, pointing to the scampering cat. "I think he's running away."

"Good riddance," Jeremy said. "That's the sneakiest-acting cat I've ever seen. Maybe he's going back to his owner."

Jane had watched until Star was out of sight. Jeremy was right. It would be better if the cat never came back.

*　　*　　*

There was no one in the Chamber of Horrors when Jane entered, but she could hear a group of eighth graders giggling and chattering in the next room.

They'd already been in there. There was a bubble gum wrapper on the floor to prove it.

Well, this is it. Jane took a deep breath and walked over to the witch-hanging exhibit, her heart pounding. *The criminal returning to the scene of the crime.*

All she had to do was slip the ring back onto Damaris's finger. And then she'd be free. Free!

The scene looked exactly as she remembered it. The cold-eyed judge. The witch with her bound, outstretched hands. The black cat at her feet.

But wait—was she imagining it, or did the cat look different somehow?

His eyes seemed more alive. More alert and watchful.

Jane shook her head. She was doing it again. Sam and Jeremy were right. She *did* have a wild imagination.

She moved closer to the statue of Damaris, pulling the ring from her back pocket.

Jane looked into the green glass of Damaris's eyes and froze.

She could feel something passing between them—between herself and the statue of the dead witch. An unspoken command. A command that Jane was powerless to refuse.

71

Jane couldn't remember leaving the museum, but she suddenly found herself in the crowded mall.

She shook her head in disbelief. What had happened? Had she been dreaming? Where was she? She looked around.

She was sitting on a bench overlooking the Cactus Court. Next to her, a mother was pointing out the blooming plants to her little boy, reading the Latin names for them from little signs stuck in the sand. He was bored and sulky and kept kicking the bench.

Everything seemed so normal. People walking by the stores. The hum of voices. The scent of pizza from the food court.

She stood up and felt in her back pocket for the ring. There it was. She'd never returned it.

She wasn't surprised. Somehow it seemed right to still have the ring, because the witch had said—

Jane screwed her eyes shut and tried to remember just what it was the witch had said. It was no use. She remembered looking into Damaris's eyes, and after that everything was a blank.

Suddenly it came to her. The witch had commanded her to do something, and she'd agreed. Yes, that was it.

She'd agreed. But to what?

The familiar dreamlike feeling of unreality came creeping over her.

72

Jeremy and Sam were sitting on the porch, waiting for her when she got home.

"Practice was canceled," Jeremy reported. "We could have gone with you after all."

"How'd it go?" Sam asked. "We've been worried."

"Fine," Jane lied. "It went just fine."

"You're sure nobody saw you return the ring?" Jeremy asked.

"No. I was alone."

"Well, I'm glad that's over," Jeremy said. He tossed the baseball he was holding from one hand to the other. "You really scared us with all that spooky talk."

"Are you *really* okay now, Jane?" Sam asked, looking at her intently. "You look kind of pale."

Jane met his gaze squarely, her eyes wide and innocent. "I'm fine, really. I was afraid someone would see me return the ring, that's all. But no one did, and now everything's okay."

She started to wheel her bike toward the garage but stopped and turned.

"Thanks, guys. For everything."

When Jane went back up to her room, the black cat was sitting on her bed. He looked up as she came in, then turned away and started to wash one paw.

Somehow she'd known he would be there. Waiting.

Fourteen

"So that nasty cat's come back," Jeremy said after supper, carrying a handful of silverware from the table to the sink. "I was hoping he was gone for good."

Star sat in the corner by his bowl. Watching. Listening.

"I guess he likes it here," Jane said. She bent over the bowl. "Yuck. This thing needs a good washing."

"The fact that Star came back is a good sign," Sam said cheerfully. "If there really *had* been something weird going on, he would have disappeared when you returned the ring."

"I guess that's one way of looking at it," Jeremy said. "This proves he's just an ordinary old cat. Hey, Sam, is there room in the dishwasher for another plate?"

It was Friday, and Sam was sleeping over. He and Jeremy planned on spending the night downstairs in the den, in their sleeping bags, watching old movies on the late show.

Right then he was helping the twins clean up the kitchen. It was their night for kitchen duty.

Jane could feel the ring against her skin as she moved about the kitchen. She'd put it on the chain again and was wearing it around her neck. It seemed almost a part of her now. Maybe that was what the witch had told her to do in the museum—to wear the ring.

It was tucked beneath her turtleneck sweater. The boys would never see it there. Besides, they believed her when she said she'd taken it back to the museum. They trusted her. Why shouldn't they? Jane had never lied to them before.

"Don't stay up too late, kids," Mrs. Hanifin said when she went up to bed. "And turn down the volume on the TV, okay? Your father has to get up early tomorrow morning."

Jeremy and Sam were in the den, watching *The Ghost of Horror Castle,* but Jane was too frightened to watch a horror movie.

She went upstairs to her room and turned on her radio. She flipped on the overhead light as well as her bedside lamp and pulled out some magazines.

This was no time to be going to sleep. For the past three days scary dreams and voices had been coming to her at night. Jane wasn't about to let it happen again.

The music on the radio was coming through a haze of static. Jane sat on the floor with her back leaning against the bed. She opened one of the magazines and tried to read. But the light in the room seemed to be getting fuzzy.

Why am I fighting this? Jane thought. *Damaris is strong. And she won't stop until she gets what she wants.*

Jane couldn't remember the last time she'd gotten a full night's rest. She felt a storm of sleep swirling around her, spiraling, then closing in. She let her head fall back onto the bed, and her shoulders and neck relaxed against the bedspread.

Almost immediately she began to dream of Damaris. The witch was standing outside on the front lawn. Fire shot up around her, making the whole yard seem to dance in its flickering shadows.

Jane could feel the heat against her face. Damaris laughed softly and raised one arm, pale and gray next to the bright flames. Her green eyes had never looked so joyous, so inviting. She beckoned to Jane with her outstretched arm. With her other hand she pressed down on the tips of the flames, and they subsided at once.

"It is time," Damaris whispered.

Jane knew what she had to do. She hurried down the stairs to the front hall and fumbled in the dark for the key that hung next to the door. Then, with an impatient shove, she pushed the door open.

Damaris was still out there, standing in the middle

76

of the lawn. As Jane went toward her she could feel the heat of the fire on her skin.

The witch's green eyes were sparkling with excitement.

"Go to the Matthewses' house," she ordered. "When you get there, you will know what to do." Suddenly Damaris strode forward and grabbed Jane's arm. She was tugging on it, calling out her name.

"Jane, Jane, wake up!"

Then it was Jeremy's voice Jane was hearing. Jeremy stood next to her in the darkness. He was shaking her.

The fire seemed to have gone out, but Jane could still smell smoke in the damp night air. The front door was open, and Sam was standing in the doorway, watching the twins anxiously.

Jeremy led Jane back into the house. They went into the den, and Jane sat on the sofa with a thick, warm afghan wrapped around her shoulders.

"You were sleepwalking," Jeremy said. "Were you having another nightmare?"

Jane's teeth were chattering. "It . . . it was Damaris," she said. "She was calling me." Her eyes were huge and dark in the dim light, and her voice trembled.

She stopped and buried her face in her hands. The afghan fell off her shoulders.

"What did she want, Jane?" Sam asked gently. "You can trust us."

Jane lowered her hands, clasping them tightly in

front of her. "She wanted me to go to Suzanne's house and . . . and do something to hurt her."

"In the middle of the night?" Jeremy said.

"It had something to do with fire, I think, because I . . . I heard the crackle of flames when Damaris was laughing. I could see it all around her."

She reached out and grabbed Jeremy by the arm. "You've got to help me. Damaris's hold on me is getting stronger."

"Hey, what's this?" Jeremy peered at the chain around Jane's neck. He pulled on it, and the ring appeared.

He stared hard at Jane, frowning. "You said you took the ring back."

"I lied," Jane said forlornly. "I do all sorts of things now that I've never done before. I've tried to really hurt Suzanne. Please don't make me tell you anything more about it. All I can say is, I caught myself just in time. But I don't know how long I can go on like this."

"But you were all set to return the ring," Sam said. "What happened?"

"I don't know. I can't remember. That's what scares me. I don't even remember leaving the museum." Jane leaned forward and continued in a low, intense voice, "The last thing I remember is looking into Damaris's eyes—the statue's eyes—and all the rest is blank." She started to cry. "She won't let me return it. And she's making me wear it around my neck. I don't know what to do!"

Jeremy and Sam stared silently at each other. Then suddenly Jeremy moved. He reached over and jerked the chain and the ring off Jane's neck.

Jane gasped and put her hand to her throat. "Don't, Jeremy! It might happen to you now."

"No, it won't," Jeremy said firmly, going over to the fireplace. "I'm going to put this thing away until tomorrow. We—all three of us—are going to that wax museum first thing in the morning to return it. Your problems all started with this dumb ring. They're going to end tomorrow, when we give it back."

Jeremy pulled a loose brick from the hearth. It was a hiding place he and Jane had discovered years before. No one knew about it but them and Sam.

He poked the chain and the ring inside and replaced the brick. "We'd better get rid of the chain, too—just in case."

Sam groaned. "Wait a minute. We can't go to the museum tomorrow. Tomorrow's our class field trip. We're going to the state park to check out the plants and wildlife, remember?"

"So we skip it," Jeremy said, standing up and brushing off the knees of his pajamas. "This is more important."

"We can't," Jane said in a hollow voice. "We get a grade for this trip."

Jeremy thought for a moment. "Then we'll return the ring *after* the trip. The museum will be open late.

In the meantime, the ring's put away where it can't do any harm. And Sam and I are going to keep our eyes on you every minute. Okay?"

"Okay," Jane said, nodding. "But do you guys mind if I spend the rest of the night here on the sofa?"

"Be our guest," Jeremy said with a sweeping gesture.

"Don't worry, Jane," Sam told her, tucking the afghan around her feet. "Everything's going to be fine."

As she dropped off to sleep, Jane remembered the cat. He hadn't been in the den with them.

This was one conversation he wouldn't be able to carry back to his mistress.

Maybe.

Fifteen

Mr. Sparks and Ms. Kramer, the science teachers, stood under a tree calling out names as the children filed off the bus.

"Okay," Mr. Sparks announced, "Kelly and Beth, over here. Greg and Mark. Ann and Karen . . ."

Ms. Kramer raised her arm and waggled her clipboard. "Please keep the noise down. We're using the buddy system, so everybody listen up for the name of your partner."

"Jeremy and Sam," continued Mr. Sparks.

Pam and Jane stood next to each other. They always tried to be partners on field trips, just as Jeremy and Sam did.

"Suzanne and Jane," called out Mr. Sparks. He stopped and consulted his list. "That's funny," he said with a puzzled frown. "I could have sworn I'd paired you two off with other people. Well, I guess it doesn't matter."

But it does. I'm afraid to be paired with Suzanne, Jane thought.

Suzanne turned and scowled at Jane, her expression cold.

Jane raised her hand. "Can I change partners, Mr. Sparks? Can Pam and I please go together?"

"Yes, Mr. Sparks," Suzanne chimed in. "I'd rather be someone else's partner, too."

"Wait a minute," Mr. Sparks said, running his hand through his thin blond hair and checking his roster again. "Okay, Jane, you can go with Pam if her partner will go with Suzanne."

"No fair!" cried Megan Levy, Pam's partner. "I had to go with Suzanne on the zoo trip and she got us lost!"

"I did not!" Suzanne shot back shrilly.

"Well, if *they* get to change, then I want to go with Ashley," called out Sarah Peters, a short blond girl with big glasses.

"What do you mean, I got us lost at the zoo, Megan?" Suzanne demanded, her hands on her hips.

Ms. Kramer blew a little brass whistle that hung from a cord around her neck. "Whoa!" she shouted.

She looked over pityingly at Mr. Sparks. He was a new teacher and was always in trouble. "Under the circumstances," she said, "I think it would be best if we all stuck to our original partners."

"But—" protested Jane.

"No ifs, ands, or buts," Ms. Kramer said in a high, clear voice. "We go by the original roster, and that's final."

"Oh, great," Suzanne muttered sarcastically. "I get Jane Hanifin, my most favorite person in the whole world!"

Ms. Kramer gave another little toot on her whistle. "Okay, line up with your partner and let's get going."

A park ranger joined the class and showed them a map of the park, explaining how all the trails led to the picnic area.

"It's impossible to get lost if you stay on the footpaths," he told them. "Just follow the paths and you'll all come out at the picnic area."

Then Ms. Kramer took over again. "We will divide up into groups now, class. Each group will take a different footpath. We will all meet at the picnic area in exactly one hour to eat our lunches and report on the different plants and birds we have seen on our nature walk. I am appointing one person to be in charge of each group. Remember, stay on the paths."

Jane and Suzanne were at the end of the line when their group started out. Jane had wanted to be up front, right behind Jeremy and Sam, but at the last minute Suzanne had realized she'd left her lunch on the bus and had to go back for it.

Jeremy and Sam were at the head of the line, right behind the group leader. Jane waved to them, signaling for them to fall back and walk with her and Suzanne, but Jeremy just waved back cheerfully.

He must think I'll be okay because I'm not wearing the ring and because there are all these kids around, she thought. *I hope he's right.*

And yet, even without the ring, Jane felt that old, familiar anger at Suzanne. Everything Suzanne did irritated her, right down to the way she was chewing her bubble gum—with her front teeth, like a chipmunk.

She and Suzanne were soon lagging behind the rest of the group. First Suzanne got a pebble in her shoe, and it took forever for her to get her shoelace unknotted. Then she had to stop and brush her hair because she'd snagged it on a bush.

Finally Jane realized that the others were no longer in sight.

"We're the last ones, Suzanne. We have to catch up. Can't you walk faster?"

"I can't help it," Suzanne snapped. "I'm getting a blister."

Jane threw her hands up in the air. "Great. Just great. So what am I supposed to do, carry you?"

Suzanne tossed back her long red hair and smiled. "I've got a better idea," she said. "I know a shortcut that will get us to the picnic area ahead of our group."

"But they'll notice we're missing," Jane protested.

"No, they won't. Ms. Kramer put that dweeb Virgil

84

Brewster in charge of our group. He won't even know we're gone."

"Wait a minute, Suzanne!" Jane called, but it was too late. Suzanne had already disappeared into the underbrush. Jane plunged in after her.

She found herself in a deep, dark wood. The sunlight filtered weakly through the overhanging branches of the trees, which met and intertwined over her head.

Jane struck off in the direction she was sure Suzanne had taken. "Suzanne?" she called. "Where are you? Wait for me."

Somewhere a bird uttered a mournful cry. There was a flutter of wings off to her right, and then silence.

"Suzanne!" Jane called, her voice trembling. "Suzanne, where are you? Where did you go?"

Her voice sounded strange in the eerie silence.

Had something happened to Suzanne?

What should she do now?

Sixteen

"Suzanne?" Jane called again.

She gasped with fright as Suzanne popped out from behind a tree.

"Here I am," Suzanne said with a smug smile. "Did you think you were lost?"

Jane's heart was thumping. "No, but I was afraid you were." She looked around. "Are you sure this is a shortcut?"

"I know this place like the back of my hand," Suzanne boasted. "My folks used to bring Gordie and me here all the time. Just follow me."

They moved on farther into the woods, pushing aside branches to clear their way. The trees were closer and closer together, and the sunlight had all but disappeared.

Jane noticed that Suzanne had stopped bragging about how well she knew the woods. In fact, she wasn't saying much at all now.

Finally Jane stopped walking and said, "We're nowhere near the picnic area, Suzanne. We're just going deeper and deeper into the woods. We're lost. Admit it."

"Maybe we should go that way," Suzanne said, pointing hesitantly to the right, her voice quavering. "Yeah, that's it. I think. Maybe."

Jane suddenly felt a wave of certainty sweeping over her. A minute before, she'd been sure she was lost. Now she knew exactly where to go and what to do. And now she realized that everything—the events of the past several days, even Mr. Sparks's pairing her with Suzanne this morning—had all been leading up to this. This moment.

Even without the witch's ring, she felt that strange, familiar dizziness coming over her again, and she heard a voice—Damaris's voice—chanting:

> Wicca, ecca, astaramus
> Wicca, ecca, tremilamus
> Mist that hides the light of sun
> Help me and this deed is done.

"I know where we are, Suzanne," Jane heard herself say coldly. "We go that way—toward that fallen tree, see?"

"But I thought you said you'd never been here before," protested Suzanne, picking a couple of twigs out of her long hair.

"I was wrong," Jane told her. "I know this place."

"And you know where the picnic area is from here?" Suzanne asked eagerly.

"I know where we're supposed to go," Jane replied in a flat voice.

"Great!" said Suzanne, a wide, relieved smile on her face. "If we hurry, we can still beat everyone else."

Jane led the way, walking stiffly, like a robot, her arms at her sides.

Behind her, Suzanne babbled on and on about how she usually didn't get lost and what a great sense of direction she had. But Jane heard only the voice in her head. The little, musical voice that kept up its soft urgent chanting:

> Mist that hides the light of sun
> Help me and this deed is done.

As if in answer to the rhyme, a ground mist had risen by the time they reached the fallen tree. It was swirling around their ankles in tattered, ragged patches as they made their way through the stands of trees that grew thinner and thinner as they moved forward.

"Oh, good!" Suzanne said, her voice brighter and more cheerful now. "We're coming out of the woods! But where did this fog come from? Isn't it creepy? I'm glad we're—"

She broke off abruptly.

The wooded area had opened out onto a small

pond. A wooden sign, stuck in the ground and tilting slightly, said in faded letters WITCH DUCK POND.

"Where are we?" Suzanne demanded. "This won't lead us to the picnic area. I thought you knew where you were going!"

"I do," Jane said in the same flat voice.

"But where are we?" Suzanne repeated, her voice high and shrill. "I've never heard of this place."

"This is where they sewed Damaris up in a sack and threw her into the water," Jane said, her eyes wide and unseeing.

"What are you talking about?" Suzanne cried. "Are you crazy, Jane?"

"The hanging judge was *your* ancestor. You should know this place better than I do," Jane answered.

The mist swirled higher around them. It was knee-high now. The afternoon sun went behind a cloud as the mist spread its long, ragged fingers over the surface of the pond.

"I . . . I think maybe we took a wrong turn somewhere," Suzanne faltered.

Wicca, ecca, astaramus . . . The chanting was all around them now.

"Jane, Jane—look over there!" Suzanne said in a hoarse whisper, pointing to the pond. "What's happening?"

The wisps of fog had drifted together in the center of the pond and now were swirling and rising up in a slender column.

As they watched, the column began to take form. Human form.

It was a woman—a tall, slim woman dressed in filmy, ghostly white.

Damaris!

Her arms reached out and beckoned to them. No, not to them. To Suzanne.

Damaris floated over the surface of the water. She shook the fog from her long black hair and smiled.

"Come to me! Come to me!" Her pale lips silently formed the words.

She beckoned again. Suzanne whimpered helplessly. "Please don't hurt me. I wasn't even there at your trial. I don't know anything about it."

Damaris snickered. "Did it matter to anyone whether *I* was guilty or innocent? Does it matter to me whether *you* are?"

Suzanne was silent. She stopped whimpering and looked deeply into the witch's mocking eyes.

Jane felt as if she'd been turned to stone. She couldn't speak or move.

Something soft and warm brushed against her leg. Jane didn't have to look down to see what it was. She knew. It was Star, the black cat. Damaris's cat.

The cat purred contentedly. Jane could hear the sound clearly in the misty silence, even when he left her side and stalked slowly, regally, down to the water's edge.

He turned and sat, his tail raised and waving gently.

He was waiting. Waiting for Suzanne.

Suzanne stirred and took an unsteady step forward. Then another. She seemed to be in a hypnotic trance. Jane tried to call out to her, to tell her to stop, but she was still frozen in place and couldn't move or speak, no matter how hard she tried.

Damaris beckoned for the third time, and Suzanne waded blindly into the pond.

Again Jane tried to move, to help Suzanne, but she couldn't. She could only watch silently as Suzanne sank up to her knees in the muddy water.

Another step, and she was up to her waist.

Sinkholes! Jane thought. *The pond must be full of sinkholes! Damaris will make Suzanne walk into one while I stand here and watch her drown. That's my punishment for taking off Damaris's ring. For not doing what she wanted me to do at the bus stop. And for the other times I failed her, too. Maybe she'll make* me *walk into the pond next!*

Damaris moved backward, gesturing for Suzanne to follow. Suzanne took another step and went under. The waters of the pond churned as her head bobbed up and down.

Jane opened her mouth and screamed, long and loud.

91

Seventeen

"Hold on, Suzanne! We're coming!"

Jane turned. Jeremy and Sam ran past her to the water's edge.

Jeremy stood on the bank of the pond and clung tightly to Sam's outstretched arm as Sam stepped carefully into the water. Then, reaching out without letting go of Jeremy, Sam grabbed Suzanne by her shirt collar and dragged her up from the depths.

Together, the boys pulled Suzanne out of the water. She lay on the bank, moaning and gagging and coughing up muddy pond water.

"Wh-where am I?" she groaned, rolling over and sitting up. "What happened?" She put her head in her hands and shuddered.

The witch and her cat had disappeared, along with the mist. The sun was shining brightly on the waters of the pond now. A bird sang in a nearby tree.

Jane found it hard to believe that just a few short

moments before, she and Suzanne had been so completely under the witch's spell. If Suzanne hadn't been sitting in front of her at that moment, dripping pond water, Jane might have wondered if she'd imagined the entire incident.

"What happened?" Suzanne asked again. "Did I slip or something?"

"You don't remember?" Jane asked cautiously.

Suzanne frowned. "No. All I remember is going under that dirty, filthy water." She looked down at her skirt. "Eww! My clothes are all muddy. And I bet I swallowed a gallon of that stuff, too. I'll probably catch some awful disease!"

"Well, ah, what happened was that you were standing next to the water and you, uh, fell in," Jane said lamely. "But the boys pulled you out," she added hastily.

She looked over at Jeremy and Sam. "And I'm so glad you did. But what are you doing here?"

Sam had taken off his sneakers and was removing his wet socks, so Jeremy answered.

"We noticed the two of you were missing, so we came back to look for you. When we heard you screaming, we ran over as fast as we could."

"You screamed?" Suzanne asked, looking at Jane and raising her eyebrows in disbelief.

"Yes, I did," Jane replied as calmly as she could. "After all, you *were* drowning, Suzanne."

"Well, you don't have to look at me like that,"

93

Suzanne said in a hurt voice. "I mean, it's not like it was my fault or anything. You're the one who said she knew a shortcut. And now—just look at my hair! It's a good thing it's naturally curly."

While Suzanne was off behind a bush, wringing out her clothes, Jane, Jeremy, and Sam had a chance to talk.

"We saw everything when we came out of the woods," Sam said in a low voice. "The witch. The cat. At first I thought I was seeing things, but Jeremy saw them, too."

"You saw Damaris?" Jane asked.

"Yeah," Jeremy said, his face pale. "And when she—" He gulped and took a deep breath. "When the witch saw us coming, she disappeared. Just like that. Poof! So did the cat."

"Now we know what you were trying to tell us, Jane," Sam said. "You've been right all along." His face was even paler than Jeremy's. "That was the scariest thing I've ever seen in my life!"

"I couldn't do anything to stop her," Jane said bitterly. "I tried, but it was like I was glued to the ground."

"It doesn't matter now," Jeremy assured her. "Suzanne's okay. And she wouldn't be if you hadn't screamed."

"No, she isn't okay," Jane said desperately. "Damaris will only try again. She's after Gordie, too. And maybe even their parents."

She could hear Suzanne coming toward them, crashing through the underbrush, so she spoke quickly. "The thing that bothers me most is that I'm not wearing the ring. I thought it was only when I wore the ring that bad things happened. But what if the ring doesn't matter anymore? Maybe it's gone beyond that." Jane wrung her hands. "I mean, Damaris must have cast some sort of spell on Mr. Sparks's list so that Suzanne and I were paired off for the nature walk. And then she put the idea of that shortcut into Suzanne's head."

She reached out and took first Jeremy's hand and then Sam's. Her voice was low and intense.

"What if the witch has me totally in her power and will never let me go—not until Suzanne and her family are dead?"

Eighteen

When they got home that afternoon, the black cat was waiting for them on the front porch, his eyes glittering with malice and his tail switching angrily. He hissed at them as they came up the steps and then he bounded away.

"You were right about the cat, too, Jane," Jeremy said, nervously looking over his shoulder for the cat as he opened the front door. "He *is* Damaris's cat. I didn't believe you until I saw him sitting there by the pond."

Jane shuddered. "Star scares me. I don't know how he gets in and out of closed rooms the way he does, but he's always there. It's like he's *listening* to us."

A note on the refrigerator door said: *Dad and I are at the Murchisons'. Be home at five. Love, Mom.*

"Well, that answers that question," Jane said. "I was wondering how we were going to tell Mom and Dad about what happened at the pond."

"Tell Mom and Dad? Are you kidding, Jane?" Jeremy asked. "You know what they're like. They don't believe in stuff like witchcraft. They'd just say we're making it up or imagining it or something."

"But we've got to tell them sometime," Jane said miserably.

"No, you don't," Sam told her, his lips set in a tight line. "I still think it's the ring that's doing all this. Once we get rid of it, the spooky stuff will stop. I mean, that's what started it in the first place, wasn't it?"

"I hope you're right," Jane said. "I guess we'll just have to wait and see what happens when we take it back."

Jeremy opened the cookie jar and pulled out a handful of cookies. "Here," he said, passing them out. "Quick energy. Then we'd better get on over to the mall. If we hurry, we can return that ring and be back here before Mom and Dad get home."

Sam went over to the wall phone and picked up the receiver. "I'd better let my mom know I'll be sleeping over another night. I want to see what happens after we return that ring."

The mall was jammed with Saturday shoppers, but the wax museum wasn't crowded. Several groups of people were touring the Chamber of Horrors, though, so Jane, Jeremy, and Sam pretended to be looking around in the other rooms.

Mr. Thatcher, the guard, came up to them when

they were in the World of Tomorrow section.

"Haven't I seen you in here before?" he asked. "You kids must like this museum."

"We're doing a project for school," Jane said primly, amazed at how easily she could make up lies these days. "We're writing a report about how people might be living in the future."

Mr. Thatcher shook his head admiringly. "Well, good for you. I'm glad to see that some kids take their studies seriously."

He touched a finger to his hat in a salute and moved away.

They waited until they were sure the other visitors had left the Chamber of Horrors and then slipped quietly down the corridor and past the thick velvet drapes.

The room was even eerier than Jane remembered.

Before her, the rigid, staring statues of Damaris and her cat stood in the pale wash of the flickering green lights. They looked evil. Sinister. They seemed to be waiting for her.

Just the thought of facing that statue of Damaris again . . . of touching her . . .

But this time the boys were with her. Taking a deep breath, she went over to the witch-hanging scene.

Jeremy and Sam stood just behind her, hiding her movements in case someone came into the room.

"Hurry up, Jane," Jeremy urged. "Let's do this thing fast and get out of here." His breath came in ragged little bursts. Jane could tell he was as scared as she was.

She reached into her pocket for the ring. Just as she was pulling it out, Mr. Thatcher strolled through the doorway. She hastily jammed it back down.

"What's this?" he demanded. "I thought you kids were doing research in the other room."

"We were," Jane managed to say smoothly. "We decided to include some town history in the report. You know, to kind of round it out—the past, the present, and then how different life might be in the future."

Her voice squeaked a little at the end, but Mr. Thatcher didn't seem to notice. He winked at them. "Okay. I just wanted to make sure you were doing your homework, not fooling around."

"I hope he doesn't come back," she whispered when Mr. Thatcher had finally moved on.

"Do it now, Jane," Sam urged. "Go for it!"

Jane's fingers trembled violently as she pulled the ring from her pocket. She held it up toward Damaris's outstretched hands.

And dropped it.

It rolled under the rope and disappeared.

"Where did it go?" she cried, dropping to her knees and pawing at the floor. "These lights are so dim, I can't see it!" She was half sobbing under the stress of the past few days.

"Shh!" Jeremy warned. He fell to his knees beside

her. "There it is!" he whispered. "Between the judge's feet."

He stretched out on his stomach and wriggled under the rope.

"Hurry up!" Sam urged. "Someone might be coming."

"I've got it!" Jeremy panted, squirming backward, using his elbows. He sat up and held out the ring to Jane. "Here. Try again. You have to be the one to do this."

Jane took one last, quick look at the ring. That peculiar word engraved on the inside—*Zebaalak*. What did it mean? *Well, no time to wonder about it now,* she told herself.

She reached out and slipped the ring onto the waxen finger. It went on easily. Just as easily as it had come off the last time.

Jane waited for the funny, ringing silence she'd experienced when she'd taken the ring. The feeling of being in a vacuum.

Nothing.

"Nothing's happening," she said, backing away.

"Why? Is it supposed to?" Sam asked.

"No. Probably not," Jane said. "Let's get out of here."

The shadows seemed to close behind them as they left the Chamber of Horrors. Soon they were out in the mall again.

Sam and Jeremy gave each other high fives.

"Where to now?" Sam asked.

"Home," Jane said. "My stomach feels like it's tied in knots. I just want to go home."

"Now that the witch doesn't have any power over you," Sam said, "the cat should be gone, too."

But when they walked through the front door, the black cat was sitting in the hallway.

Jane felt her blood turn to ice water.

The cat purred loudly. Contentedly. He looked smug. Triumphant. Almost as if he were smiling.

"It's too late," Jane whispered, her lips trembling. "Nothing can stop it now."

Nineteen

It was Sam who came up with the idea of going to the library.

"They've got a whole section on the history of this town," he told Jane and Jeremy. "They're bound to have some books on witchcraft, too. Maybe we can figure out what's going on here. There's got to be a way out of this mess."

The library stayed open until 10:00 P.M. on Saturday night. Mr. and Mrs. Hanifin were impressed that the three of them were willing to give up a weekend evening of popcorn and videos in order to get some extra studying done.

"It's this project we have to do for school, Mom," Jane said. "It's due Monday."

She'd been telling lies so often she was almost beginning to believe this one.

"I'll pick you up at closing time, okay?" Mr. Hanifin said after supper when he dropped them off.

Jane asked the librarian for help. "We're doing a history of the town," she explained, "especially the colonial period. We need to know more about the hanging of Damaris Pearson, the witch."

Mrs. Lawrence shook her head and made a little tut-tutting sound. "That was a terrible thing," she said. "A black mark on this town's history. It's hard to believe something like that ever happened here."

"And if you have any books on witchcraft, we'd like to see them too, please," Sam put in. "You know, for background material," he added hastily.

Mrs. Lawrence went over to her computer and tapped away, jotting down notes on little pieces of paper. Then she picked up her notes and disappeared into the stacks.

"Do you think she'll be able to find anything?" Jane asked.

Jeremy reached across the library table where they were seated and patted her hand awkwardly. "Don't worry, Jane. Everything's going to be okay."

Jane put her head in her hands. "It's my own fault that I'm in this mess. And now I've got you guys mixed up in it, too. If only I hadn't taken that ring."

"It wasn't your fault, Jane," Sam said. "The ring—and its weird power—was locked up in the archives for three hundred years. Damaris waited all that time for her revenge. You just had bad luck."

"But I stole the ring," Jane began.

"From what you've said, you only *touched* the ring.

103

Damaris did the rest. She put the idea of taking it into your head. Don't be so hard on yourself."

Mrs. Lawrence finally reappeared, pushing a small library cart. The top shelf held several file folders, each one spilling over with yellowed newspaper clippings. The bottom shelf was piled with books.

"People have written about the witch-hanging from time to time over the years," she explained, stacking the folders neatly on the table. "The articles are all in these folders."

She gestured to the bottom shelf of the cart. "And here," she said, "are some books on witchcraft. There are more in the stacks if you want to look for them. Now please be careful. Some of these books and papers are quite old. I'm afraid I cannot allow you to take them out of the reference room."

The children set to work eagerly. They started with the newspaper articles. Jane divided up the folders.

The only sound in the room was the steady ticking of the old-fashioned wall clock as the three friends pored over the yellowed clippings.

"It's no use," Jeremy said at last, looking up and closing his folder. "These don't say anything new. They tell the same story that's on the sign in the wax museum."

"Mine too," Sam said. "I thought there might be something more about the cat. But these articles only say that the cat was supposed to be the witch's familiar, and that he was executed along with Damaris."

"Wait a minute," Jane said, holding up her hand. "I've found a footnote about the cat."

Her eyes skimmed across the page. Then she laid the article down, her hands trembling.

"The cat's name was Zebaalak," she said in a hollow voice.

"What about it?" Jeremy asked.

"That's the name that was engraved inside the ring," Jane explained.

"Why would she have her cat's name inside her ring?" Jeremy asked.

"Because Zebaalak wasn't—isn't—just a cat," Sam said thoughtfully. "He's her familiar. Remember my telling you that the job of a familiar was to carry out the witch's spells?"

"Yeah," Jane said, nodding. "That still doesn't explain why she—"

"Because first she needed to call him up," Sam interrupted. "To make him appear. That must be what the ring does. That was why it was so important. It has the power to call up Zebaalak, her familiar."

"But I thought it was Damaris who got called up when I took that ring," Jane said.

"No," Sam said. "Maybe she's always been here. Her dead spirit, I mean. But she couldn't do anything without her familiar."

He lowered his voice to a whisper. Jane and

Jeremy leaned closer across the table to hear him. "Being a spirit, not having a body, Damaris needed a human to do her work for her. A human who would get hold of that ring and bring the cat back to carry out her charms and spells. A human who would do the job on the Matthews family."

"And *I* had to be the one who took the ring," Jane groaned. "How dumb can you get?"

"But we returned it," Jeremy argued. "Why didn't that make the cat disappear?"

"Because he and Damaris have been getting stronger all the time. I can feel it," Jane said fearfully. "Especially after what happened today at the pond. She doesn't seem to need the ring anymore to control me." She shivered. "What if she keeps getting stronger? I think she wants to take over my body. To possess me. Maybe that's what she's planning to do, once she's destroyed Suzanne and her family."

"Then we have to get rid of the cat," Sam said. "Right now. Without him, she'll go back to being as powerless as she was before."

"But how?" Jeremy asked. "We don't know anything about witchcraft."

Jane jumped up from her chair and bent over the cart, gathering up the books on witchcraft and placing them on the table.

"Look at all these books. Mrs. Lawrence said some of them are pretty old."

She carefully opened one, then another. A strong,

musty odor arose as she paged through them. The paper was brown and dry, and the printing was faded.

"Wow, these things must go way back," she said. "The pages look even older than the covers. They must have been rebound at some time. And look," she said, pointing to what looked like a primitive illustration of a witch stirring something in a pot, "they've even got charms and recipes for potions."

"What are books like *these* doing in our library?" Jeremy asked, his eyes wide.

Sam picked up a book and blew dust off the cover. "I'll bet the librarians don't know what's in them. Lots of libraries have books on witchcraft. But these must be the real thing!"

"Good," Jane said, dividing the books up among them. "Maybe we can find something in one of them telling us how to get rid of a black cat."

"I can't believe I'm spending Saturday night in the library, looking for charms and magic potions," Jeremy said.

"Believe it," Jane ordered. "And start reading. The library closes at ten."

They were still searching desperately through the books an hour later when Mrs. Lawrence appeared. "The library closes in fifteen minutes," she said. "I have to start gathering up the reading material now."

"Oh, please, Mrs. Lawrence," Jane begged. "Just a

few minutes more. It's taking us longer to go through these books than we thought."

"Well, all right, dear," Mrs. Lawrence said. "I'll make an exception in your case. It really is unusual to see children as interested in research as you three are."

Jane was aware of every tick of the clock as its hands crept closer and closer to ten.

They had to find something that night. The library was closed the next day, Sunday. That meant Damaris and Zebaalak would have another day in which to make her do their bidding.

Five more minutes. The library lights flickered on and off, a signal that it soon would be closing.

"Wait a minute!" Jane cried. "I've found something. It's called The Spell of the Inverted Triangle. It says that it gets rid of enemies. It's worth a try, anyway."

The lights flickered their warning again.

Jane reached over and grabbed Sam's spiral notebook. "Quick, give me your pen, Sam. I have to copy this down!"

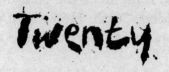

Twenty

Jane, Jeremy, and Sam were up early the next morning.

Sam and Jeremy had spent the night in the den again, in their sleeping bags. Jane had stayed on the sofa once more, but she had been too nervous to get much sleep. She had heard the boys tossing and turning, and she suspected that they hadn't slept much, either.

When morning finally came, the three friends went into the kitchen to lay their final plans.

"Are you sure Star isn't around, listening?" Jane asked. She glanced uneasily over her shoulder.

"He's still locked up in my room, where he's been all night," Jeremy told her.

"Do we have everything?" Sam asked nervously.

Jane held up a piece of white chalk and a round blue container of salt. "This is all I need. Do you have the rope, Jeremy?"

"Right here," he answered, reaching under his chair and hauling out a coil of rope. "I can hardly wait to tie up that ugly old cat."

"And do you remember the chant?" Jane asked.

Jeremy nodded. "Yeah. How about you, Sam?"

"I'll probably remember it for the rest of my life," Sam said.

Jeremy looked anxiously over at his sister. "Are you sure this will work? The charm and the Inverted Triangle thing?"

"I hope so," Jane said. "It's the only ceremony I could find that even came close to what we're looking for. If it doesn't work, I don't know what else we can do."

"It *will* work," Sam said firmly. "You've taken the ring back. You've resisted Damaris. And now we're going to get rid of Zebaalak."

"When should we do it?" Jeremy asked.

"As soon as Mom and Dad leave for Aunt Winnie's," Jane said. "Today. At high noon."

"It sounds like the gunfight at the OK Corral," Jeremy said.

"Well, it's not too different," Jane replied grimly. "The three of us against *them*."

Jane thought her parents would never leave for Aunt Winnie's.

First Mrs. Hanifin kept complaining that she couldn't do a thing with her hair. Then she couldn't decide what

110

to wear, and when she did, it needed to be ironed. When Jane finally thought her mother was ready to leave the house, Mrs. Hanifin snagged her pantyhose and had to go back upstairs to change them.

By the time her parents drove off, Jane was sure she had a good start on a nervous breakdown.

Mrs. Hanifin had released Star from Jeremy's room, and the cat was acting suspicious—skulking around, listening at doors. It was obvious he knew something was up.

Jane was determined not to let Damaris into her head. All morning she kept silently repeating the chant they would be using later, during the ceremony:

> By all the powers of earth and sea
> Get thee hence and set me free.

If Damaris was trying to get into her brain, she wouldn't have a chance, Jane figured.

Once they were sure that Mr. and Mrs. Hanifin were gone, Jane, Jeremy, and Sam swung into action.

The first thing they had to do was tie up the cat.

This was Jane's idea. "He's got to be right here in the room when we cast the spell so we can see whether or not it's working," she said.

"Okay," Jeremy said. "I'll sneak up on Zebaalak from behind and grab him. Then Sam will slip a rope around his neck. He ought to be pretty harmless after that."

But when Jeremy went to grab him, the cat fought back with his razor-sharp claws, scratching Jeremy's arms. Sam rushed forward, blocking the cat's escape route with his body. Zebaalak struggled frantically, shrieking and snarling, but Sam gripped him tightly.

"Grab the rope!" Sam gasped.

Jeremy quickly picked it up off the floor, where Sam had dropped it, and slipped it over the cat's head.

Jeremy's arms were covered with scratches and Sam's T-shirt was torn when they finally succeeded in tying the cat, writhing and spitting, to the foot of a tall old bookcase in Jeremy's room, where the ceremony would take place.

The bookcase had been chosen because it was a heavy, immovable piece of furniture made of solid oak, with thick glass doors.

"This ought to hold him, even if he does try to escape," Jeremy said.

Once they were sure the cat was secure, they pushed Jeremy's bed closer to the wall and rolled up the rug, leaning it against the side of the bookcase.

Zebaalak hissed and struggled as they made their preparations. But when Jane took out the piece of white chalk and knelt on the floor, he fell silent, his eyes slitted and menacing.

"Do you have the salt?" Sam asked in a hoarse whisper.

"Yeah, it's right here," Jeremy whispered back, holding up the container.

112

Jane looked up at them solemnly, her hand grasping the chalk tightly, poised to write. "Are we ready?"

The boys nodded. Jeremy chewed on his bottom lip.

"Okay, then. Let's go," Jane said.

And then from downstairs, like a clap of doom, Mrs. Hanifin's clear, high soprano voice floated up to them. "Hey, kids! Did I leave my purse up there?"

"It's Mom!" Jane jumped up and ran to the door. "She's back!"

She ran down the stairs to head off her mother.

"Wouldn't you know it," Mrs. Hanifin was complaining, her foot on the bottom stair. "We were almost at Winnie's house when I realized I'd left my purse at home. Have you seen it, Jane?"

"I-It's over there on the hall table," Jane stammered. "I can see it from here."

Mrs. Hanifin smacked her forehead with the flat of her hand. "I swear, I'd forget my head if it weren't attached to my body." She walked over to the table and picked up her handbag, throwing the strap over one shoulder. "Thanks, sweetie. I'd better run. Your father is having an absolute fit about having to come back. We're a half hour late already."

Jane locked the door behind her mother and trudged back upstairs, her legs weak and trembling.

"She's gone," she told the boys. "That was close. Now let's do it!"

The cat tugged wildly at his tether, fangs bared, as Jane knelt and chalked the Inverted Triangle version of Zebaalak's name—the name over and over again, dropping a letter each time, to make him fade away, just like the word:

Zebaalak
Zebaala
Zebaal
Zebaa
Zeba
Zeb
Ze
Z

She rose and looked down at her work. "There it is," she said softly, putting the chalk back in her pocket. "The Inverted Triangle. And now we walk Widdershins."

They had learned about the Widdershins spell in the old book of charms at the library. It involved walking counterclockwise around the Inverted Triangle.

But first Jane and Sam held out their hands, and Jeremy poured salt into their cupped palms. They were supposed to throw salt over their left shoulders as they walked.

As Jeremy poured out the salt a terrible smell began to fill the room.

It was the smell of sulfur. And something else—the smell of the grave.

Damaris!

Was the witch there, unseen, watching?

A feeling of total hopelessness came over Jane. Why was she doing this? What was the use? What good would it do? But then she realized suddenly, *This feeling hit me at the same time I noticed that awful smell of the grave. It's Damaris, trying to make me stop the charm. But I won't!*

"Keep going!" Jane told the boys, squaring her shoulders.

Zebaalak snarled and shrieked as they began to walk in a counterclockwise circle around the chalked triangle, throwing salt over their left shoulders and chanting, "By all the powers of earth and sea, get thee hence and set me free."

They would have to complete the circle nine times.

The cat's yowling grew louder and wilder.

Jane's heart was thumping so hard, she was afraid it would burst right out of her body. She could tell the boys were frightened, too. Their voices quavered slightly as they chanted, but they kept going. Their determination gave her fresh courage.

Three more times.

Two more times.

Then they started the ninth and last turning.

Jane had only a small pinch of salt left to throw over her shoulder as she began her final Widdershins.

As she passed the cat for the last time, he uttered

an unearthly screech that made the hairs on the back of her neck stand straight up. She stopped dead, unable to go forward.

At once the shimmering, barely distinct form of Damaris appeared beside the black cat. It took on body. Substance.

And then there she was.

Damaris looked as she must have looked at her hanging. The heavy noose was around her slender white neck. Her green eyes were furious. Glaring. Evil.

Slowly, slowly she raised her bound hands . . . and pointed to Jane.

Damaris opened her mouth to speak.

Jane knew what was coming next. A curse. A curse upon her, her family, and her future children.

Jeremy hit her in the back. Hard. "Go, Jane!" he cried. "Move! Now!"

"By all the powers of earth and sea, get thee hence and set us free!" Sam shouted.

Jeremy pushed Jane, throwing salt over his shoulder. "Go!" he yelled again.

"No!" Damaris shrieked. "No!" She held up her hands. "No," she repeated in a softer, more coaxing tone.

Jane hesitated, held captive by Damaris's hypnotic green eyes.

Jeremy punched her as hard as he could in the arm.

Still she didn't move.

Damaris's hands were raised.

Jane stared into those eyes. She was a slave to Damaris's bidding.

Then Jeremy threw what was left of his salt in Damaris's direction.

"Keep going, Jane!" he shouted, punching her in the upper arm with his knuckles.

Jane winced with pain.

"No! Stop!" Damaris commanded silently.

Jane hesitated, her mind whirling.

Then she remembered Suzanne in the pond. How she'd stepped into the sinkhole and nearly drowned.

I shall come back to destroy your children, Damaris had said to Judge Matthews.

The museum, the ring, and the tableau of the hanging all seemed to merge.

"Jane!" Sam shouted. "Move!"

Damaris's eyes glittered.

Jane forced herself to take a step. Her feet felt leaden, as if she were pulling her legs through quickly drying cement.

Damaris's image began to fade like smoke in a breeze. "No!" she shrieked helplessly.

Her voice grew softer, more distant.

And then Damaris was gone. Gone without a trace, her curse unspoken.

Jane threw down her last bit of salt. Only a few more steps now and the final Widdershins would be completed.

And then, suddenly, there was a loud crash as Zebaalak, pulling against his tether, upended the heavy oak bookcase and sent it crashing to the floor, knocking the doors off and shattering the glass.

As they watched in horror and amazement, the cat sprang straight up into the air, to the length of his rope, toward them . . . and disappeared.

Long minutes passed as Jane, Jeremy, and Sam stared at the empty air and the rope lying on the floor.

Finally Jane sank back on the bed, every limb trembling. Even her jaw was wobbling. She tried to hold it steady with both hands, but it was no use.

The boys collapsed onto the floor.

Three pale faces stared blindly at each other.

"They're . . . they're gone," Jane managed to say. "It's over."

"It worked," Sam said weakly. "It really worked."

Another long, silent moment. And then—

"Do you—" Jeremy's voice came out as a high-pitched squeak. He cleared his throat and tried again. "Do you think that old witchcraft book has a charm that will let me hit nothing but home runs this season?"

Twenty-One

The next day, the following article appeared in the local paper:

MYSTERY AT WAX MUSEUM
MUSEUM OWNERS PUZZLED

Owners of the recently opened Rappaport's House of Wax are trying to discover what caused the mysterious meltdown of two of their wax figures yesterday afternoon.

"It must have happened quickly. I'd been in there earlier, and everything looked fine," stated Morris Rappaport, one of the owners. "The next time I checked, the figures were melted right down to the ground. It couldn't have been vandalism. The museum was closed at the time."

"The melted figures were from one of our

most popular scenes," said his brother, Oscar Rappaport, the co-owner of the museum. "They were those of the witch and her black cat, from the witch-hanging tableau, taken from local history."

"We've had other strange happenings with that tableau," added his brother. "The ring the model was wearing, which belonged to the real witch, disappeared a few days ago and then suddenly reappeared. We're happy to say that the meltdown did not harm the ring."

The owners went on to say that they plan to re-create the tableau, and that the ring will still be on exhibit to add that touch of witch's magic to bewitch and enchant their viewers.